A Ghost of a Chance

by
Evelyn Klebert

A Ghost of a Chance
By Evelyn Klebert

A Cornerstone Book
Published by Cornerstone Book Publishers

First Cornerstone Edition - 2005
Second Cornerstone Edition - 2019
Third Cornerstone Edition - 2024

Cornerstone Book Publishers
Hot Springs Village, AR
www.cornerstonepublishers.com

ISBN: 978-1-61342-162-8

Dedication

For my husband,

my reason

Table of Contents

A Ghost of a Chance

Prologue

*I*s there a connective thread in everything that happens in someone's life?

He checked his watch for about the seventh time since he'd flown out of the door of his fourteenth-floor Manhattan apartment. In ten minutes, he was due across town for a meeting. He paced in front of the elevator door. Usually, it was slow, but today, it was interminable when he desperately needed everything to fly — just to fly.

Those things that you can never anticipate—was it all chance or the product of some grand cosmic design?

"Where are you, Jack? Mr. Braseman has called three times already. You were supposed to prep him before the meeting?"

"I'm just flagging down a cab. Everything's going haywire. My alarm didn't wake me, and my cell phone was turned off." He rubbed his eyes. He'd overslept but felt like he hadn't slept at all. "Tell him I got caught in a traffic jam."

"Jack, he sounded really upset."

"Look, Bev, there's nothing I can do. Stall him. I'll be there."

He hung up — just didn't want to hear anymore. He was out of breath. Down the street, there was already heavy traffic, but he couldn't spot any cabs. The city was usually glutted with them. But not as far as his eyes could see, not when he needed one.

He stopped. He had to — for a minute, to breathe again. He looked up. The skyscrapers over his head stretched into the clouds.

The questions, the big ones, admittedly, he hadn't taken much time to ponder.

After all, such issues fell into the philosophical arena — again, where he hadn't cared to spend much time. There weren't any clear-cut answers on this stuff written down in a book. Well, maybe some book, but not his brand of reading material — the stock market, law journals, and Agatha Christie novels. They were his Achilles heel. He'd always felt that Agatha did have her hand on the pulse of human nature.

"Brennan, where are you? Your receptionist gave me this number. I've invested too much in your firm to have you screw this deal up for me." Click

"Jack, hi, it's Tessa Knowles. Remember we met last weekend? Um, Bob Walters introduced us at the Peterson reception. Anyway, Bob tells me you don't slow down for anybody, so I decided to call you. My number is 23—"

He clicked the phone off. That was all the messages. He loosened his tie. It was hot, unusually hot, even for an August day. It was getting to him — the heat, really beginning to get to him.

He peered down the street anxiously. Damn it, again, no cabs in sight, people were everywhere, even this early, but it wasn't early.

He rechecked his watch. It was late. People standing with him near the street, looking, hungry for a cab, hungry to get somewhere.

He was young, he thought, only thirty-five. One would think that statistically, he had a better chance of being knifed by a mugger. But the time of death has little or, better said, nothing to do with statistics or probability. It was simply the time.

Finally, a cab was coming down the street, but three other people were already starting in that direction. He moved to enter the race but just couldn't — must stop, just a second, just to breathe.

"The water's always the place I go to recharge, son. It makes everything slow down and make sense." He was with his father again out on the fishing boat, just for a second, one precious second.

But the noise, the loud noises of the city, rushed up and dragged him back.

Shouldn't momentous days be filled with momentous things instead of little things?

Across the street, he saw steam rising off the hot cement sidewalk. Someone was murmuring near him about an Italian restaurant they wanted to try for lunch. And on top of it all, the gasoline fumes from the street traffic burned his nose and throat. He couldn't draw the air in. And all he needed was a moment to breathe.

Too quickly came the crushing pain in his chest, his knees buckling, refusing to support him further, and the merciful, dizzying blackness.

It did seem that he was unjustly young. He was only thirty-five, but on that hot August morning, for some odd reason, Jack Brennan wasn't terribly surprised.

CHAPTER ONE

Ha||ie

Hallie Barkly was a writer of horror stories, or rather horror novels, and had achieved some moderate success in her profession. Of course, only some knew that they were her books at all. The first one she had ever published, her own mother refused to believe was hers. "Why on earth, darling, would a beautiful young woman like you write such convoluted and horrible things? You've always been such a lovely, kind, considerate child. Why, you even came out of that unfortunate divorce from Edward so, well, benevolent. Where on earth did all this twisted rage come from?"

And Hallie had smiled and said little, unwilling to argue this point or any other with her mother. Where did this rage come from? Where indeed? Edward, however, did figure prominently in the works of Sebastian Winters, Hallie's dark and proactive pseudonym.

Her ex-husband made his debut appearance as the manipulative and self-absorbed lawyer who gets butchered in *Vengeance's Angel* and then later the anal accountant who gets his just due in *Requiem for the Midnight Hour*. She had to admit that it did feel good to oft the son of a bitch, at least in her mind. Because in the real world, she hadn't said boo to his unfair machinations in their divorce settlement. But then again, all that repressed frustration he had cultivated did give birth to a well-sustained career as Sebastian Winters. And, in some fashion, had also led her here to seclusion.

RRrrrrng. She picked up the phone she'd carelessly tossed on her well-cluttered computer desk. Without hesitation, she answered. There were only a handful of people who actually knew where she was. "Hello?"

"Hallie, it's Monica. I've been trying to reach you for several days."

"Oh, I'm sorry. I haven't been checking my voicemail."

"Or email?"

"Yeah, well, I got on a roll with the novel, so—" She strummed her jagged, unmanicured nails on the desk, dubiously reflecting on how untrue that particular statement was.

"I was a little worried about you." Dramatic pause, "You know, being so isolated, moving out alone in the country."

"It's just for the summer, Monica, so I can write this book."

"Another vampire book?" She smiled vaguely, distressed by the awkward collection of words on the screen.

"Yes, but this one will be different," the statement perhaps more to herself than Monica.

"Will you promise to drive into the city this weekend to have lunch with me? I haven't been able to get away. Things are popping here."

"A marketing emergency?"

"Well, we all can't be successful authors of pulp fiction."

Her voice had gotten a little testy. Evidently, Hallie had unknowingly ticked her off again. "I see you still hold my work in high regard."

"No, no, in my book, success is success, no matter what you do to get it. Anyway, you know I'm just jealous."

She tapped her fingers nervously on the desk. She wasn't in the proper frame of mind for Monica's backhanded compliments. Her mind was too caught up in struggling with her problematic narrative. "Well, don't be. You have a life. All I have is what's in my head."

"And from what I gather, that's a rather grisly place to be."

"Yes, well, I can't deny that. Look, I'll call you at the end of the week."

"Will you?"

"Promise."

"I don't like the way you sound. Give Sebastian a rest for a while, like an everlasting one."

"Oh, very good. Bye, hang up now."

She was odd and, for lack of a better word, quirky. It was a description that he wasn't ordinarily apt to use. That was his first impression of her. In addition, she was really kind of a slob. Her office was a disaster. This drove him crazy, or at least it used to. He needed order around him to think and to plan strategies. But now everything felt disconnected. Priorities had somehow radically shifted all over the place.

Of course, it took him a while to realize she really couldn't see him. In fact, she wasn't aware of him at all. They occupied the same house, sometimes almost the same place, but Hallie Barkly was completely oblivious to his presence.

He had unearthed this particular truth amid a few embarrassing encounters. Coming to the old house had been like waking up from an extended sleep. He was groggy and disoriented. He was even wearing the same dark navy suit that he'd remembered putting on that morning. And then she'd come in the room and walked right by him.

Understandably startled, he'd stammered, "Excuse me, can you please tell me where I am?" silence. "Miss, don't you hear me? I have no idea how I got here." And then, as she crossed through the room again, "What's your problem? Are you deaf?" He followed her around for a while and eventually gave up, dubiously accepting that he was not what he used to be or that she was an imbecile.

He found her name on her driver's license in her purse. He'd picked up the purse, the size of a saddlebag, and rooted through it until he found the little beige wallet stuffed to capacity.

She had some credit cards, the license, more crumpled receipts than he cared to count, and what he surmised from the resemblance was a picture of her family – two parents and one sister. The sister, he observed, looked like his unobservant housemate but had eyes that were, frankly, harder. Sizing people up was a component of Jack's success, and to him, Hallie Barkly exuded a sensitive, sort of vulnerable quality.

Of course, rather quickly, he concluded that it was probably best that they hadn't met back in New York because, on the whole, Jack hadn't been too nice to women. And, quite honestly, most of the women he'd known hadn't been too nice. He swam with sharks. In his old circle, Hallie would have been like a guppy in a tank filled with predators. But he thought these things without certainty or much conviction.

Outside of the superficial changes he'd undergone in this new realm, like the being invisible part, it was becoming clear that he was subtly and overtly linked to this woman. This became painfully obvious when he tried to leave the house on his own. It was a No-Go. The front door was like a brick wall. The farthest he could get was a screen porch on the side of the house.

It became all too clear to him that he couldn't go anywhere unless she left, too. Luckily, he'd been able to tag along when she went out to the grocery, and having raging cabin fever, he'd considered even that a treat.

So ultimately, instead of letting himself descend into panic, Jack decided to bide his time and collect information until he could act. Perhaps patience was a lesson he would be learning here if, indeed, this strange episode had any purpose. But without having any real reason to think so, he felt that somehow, in an obscure way, Hallie Barkly was his responsibility.

What exactly that meant, he didn't have a clue. Only that he was stuck in this old country house with her for some definitive reason, which he needed to unravel in order to get unstuck or until someone came along to get him out.

It was in an attempt to distract himself from all these disturbing thoughts that he'd first discovered Sebastian Winters.

His eyes were black, not the color of ebony or obsidian, but the absence of color – the void. To look into them was essentially to surrender one's soul, one's very essence, to the will of another – and alas, to be oh so grateful to do so.

He glanced across the room at Hallie intensely typing on her computer keyboard. He had settled in a gold, velvet, wing-backed chair that she had positioned in the corner of the room. She'd converted this spare bedroom into an office of sorts. In his hands, he held a paperback, one of the first Sebastian Winters novellas published by *Dark Reflection Intrigue Books*. According to the back cover, it had been number fifteen in their summer releases entitled *The Vampire's Grip*. He was scanning through the paperback, aware that he could somehow do this without Hallie's knowledge. The two of them existed often in the same space, but somehow, he suspected, not in the same flow of time. It was an awareness that had come to him, almost as though he was slowly being fed pieces of information about this new existence of his.

He continued,

Jasmine, the young, blond, cleaning woman, felt a presence within the building, although that in itself was not unusual. It was an office complex usually well populated by young yuppie executives, but it was well after regular business hours.

It wasn't impossible that someone was working late. Even as she reassured herself, she trembled with an apprehension flowing forth from an unknown source. She forced herself to continue to empty the wastepaper baskets, ignoring the sensation as well as the unduly rapid beating of her heart that she could feel pounding loudly in her chest.

Even the pulsing blood in her protrusive jugular vein seemed to swish to a new, unfamiliar rhythm.

He looked again at the intense, meek figure positioned at the monitor and grimaced. "Lovely," he murmured.

And then, as though through no will of her own, her eyes were dragged up to focus on the long corridor ahead of her.

There he stood where there was no one moments earlier – a man with Latin-like features, undeniably attractive, and yet with an unusually pale complexion.

He was dressed in a well-tailored, designer suit, but that in itself wasn't surprising. Jasmine knew that the building held an eclectic, international mix of executives.

As startling as was his sudden appearance, he was now holding out his hand toward her, beckoning and speaking her name in deliciously broken English, "Jasmine."

The very sound of her name on his lips reverberated everywhere around her. "Uh," she stammered with difficulty, "do you need your trash cans emptied?"

He spoke again in his deep, rich foreign accent, "Jasmine, come to me."

She felt herself pulled toward him, compelled, magnetized, as though nothing on earth could prevent her from going to him.

"Yes, yes, we get the idea." The intense melodrama felt acutely uncomfortable to his pragmatic mind.

And she did.

And the page ended. It was the end of a chapter. He looked up, confused. What strange drivel? He flipped to the beginning of the next chapter and glanced down the first page.

Whoah, it was jolting, disturbing, even for him. Apparently, quite a blood bath ensues after the mysterious stranger takes a chunk out of Jasmine's protruding jugular. He laughed to himself to dispel a little of the shock. How very odd for such pent-up intensity to be locked in that nearly fragile, gentile creature across the room.

She stopped typing at the computer and slumped dramatically over the desk. The sudden movement had surprised him. Drawn by curiosity, he put *The Vampire's Grip* aside and went to her.

He looked down at the back of her head resting on the desk. She did have pretty hair. It was a light brown— thick and wavy, generously highlighted with streaks of golden blonde. He'd known women who had their hair colored this way in a beauty salon, but somehow, he felt with Hallie, it was just natural. Their shared occupancy had taught him that she didn't seem to worry about externals often.

He reached out his hand to softly touch her hair, but she didn't move. She didn't know he was there. And he still didn't know why he was.

Jack didn't trust Monica Quimby. She was a tall, slender, brown-eyed blond whose features were too sharply defined by dieting, hard living, and probably working out quite often. But it was the sternness and determination set in her face that he didn't like. He'd seen it often enough. In fact, he'd dated it often enough.

"I don't know, Hallie. This place just seems kind of isolated. Aren't you worried about someone breaking in?"

Hallie smiled indulgently and sipped her cup of ridiculously hot peppermint tea.

"This isn't the big city, you know. Not much happens out here except hunting. I do hear gunshots outside sometimes."

"Oh well, that's comforting." Monica sat on the beige, overstuffed sofa that Hallie had brought from her apartment in Richmond and crossed her exceptionally long, shapely legs. She was dressed in one of her more tightly fitted business suits with a slit in the skirt long enough to facilitate movement and tantalize at the same time.

There was a time when Hallie envied her old college roommate, her looks, and her confidence. But a dose of life and experience had let her glean that Monica was a terribly restless and unhappy person. She was aggressive in going after what she wanted, but once she got it, she was never satisfied for very long.

"Honestly, Hal, moving all your stuff here for just the summer."

"Probably more like six months."

"Now it's six months. Are you ever coming back to the real world?"

"This feels pretty real to me." Jack moved to sit in a large wooden rocking chair beside the light blue lazy boy that Hallie was in. Her taste certainly was a mishmash of styles. But that didn't bother him much. She got what she liked. To him, it showed a sort of independence. She seemed calm and serene when dealing with the blonde piranha. What strange contrasts she seemed to be composed of.

Monica sighed in dramatic exasperation. "You know what I mean. When was the last time you had a date?"

"Umm, let's see. Probably when Edward asked me to marry him."

Her small green eyes got a little bigger. "Are you serious? It's been four years since your divorce. You're a successful author. You're a great catch."

"Oh good, let me get a man for those reasons. No, thank you, I don't need another fouled-up relationship."

"Come on, Hallie. A bad relationship is better than none at all."

She frowned, rubbing her forehead casually. It was the odd sensation again, a pressure just above her eyes that she felt from time to time in the house. "Do you have any idea how truly screwed up that sounds?"

"Yes, I do, but I don't want you to be alone."

"I'm not. I have Sebastian Winters with me."

"Do you have any idea how screwed up that sounds?"

She sighed with a touch of exaggeration. "Yes, strangely enough, I do. Finish your tea, then we can take a drive in the mountains."

Monica grimaced, looking dissatisfied that her point was lost on her friend. "As long as you don't drive off a mountain."

"You are cranky. Are you having your period?"

Jack rolled his eyes. This is stuff he really needed to hear.

"I don't believe you're a lost soul, Samory."

"Gabriella, you should leave now. You don't know how many I have killed over the course of my centuries of life. Your innocence cannot save me."

"No, that's not true. Love can change anyone."

Jack looked quizzically at the woman typing intently on the keyboard beside him. The large brown eyes were glazed. She seemed very tired. Of course, fatigue didn't seem to bother him anymore. The round, nautical-looking clock she'd hung on the wall read two 'o'clock. Time had ceased to be very significant for him, but Hallie should be asleep.

Then again, he had gathered that she was a bit nocturnal by nature. These late hours did seem to be a very productive time for her.

"I do love you, Samory. Our lives can begin now."

"How naive you seem, Gabriella," Jack murmured under his breath. And then, in the next moment, Hallie had typed:

"How naive you seem, Gabriella."

"Why do you say hurtful things to me, Samory?"

He smiled, intrigued by the phenomena. Now, what campy thing would a woman want to hear? Jack whispered deliberately to her, "Because it is the truth. You cannot know what a horror my existence is. I am death, living death." And in the next moment, to his delight, it was typed on the screen.

"But you can change."

Jack continued with mounting interest, "You ask me to change my essence, Gabriella. That is not possible," he paused. "I wish I had known you in my other life. Then it wouldn't have been too late for you to breathe your innocence into my jaded existence."

"What do you mean, Samory, by jaded? It couldn't have always been that way."

Jack frowned. Now, what would the vampire say? "If it wasn't, it was too long ago for me to remember."

Hallie stared at the screen, looking a little confused. *"But Samory what about the time before, before you were changed?"*

Jack considered his answer. "Well, perhaps when I was younger. Maybe there would have been a chance for me to live differently, to stop and see the beauty in life instead of just the toil." Oddly, he'd begun remembering the frustration he'd felt at his old law firm. "The endless toil at the office," he murmured distractedly. Oops, he stopped, noticing his slip, but she'd typed it.

She paused, rereading what she'd written, and spoke out loud. "The toil at the office?"

"Uh, well, I mean the long hours toiling at the castle."

She'd typed it but looked very confused. She spoke out loud, "I must be losing it."

Jack leaned near her, briefly closing his eyes, then whispering in her ear. "The truth is that I filled my life with things that I told myself were important and surrounded myself with people I thought felt the same way. But I was always lost, filled with a desire for more, something I could never find."

16

She was very still, as though she were hearing him somehow.

He knelt down and sat on the floor beside her chair. "Life is so strange. You go on day to day pushing yourself to achieve things, material things that we all prize, but then when you have them, their pleasure is so brief. It just slips through your fingers, and you're left trying, always trying to fill in the holes, but it never really works."

He stopped. He was rambling, pouring out truths about himself for no reason except that there wasn't a reason not to now. He hadn't really ever acknowledged how profoundly dissatisfied he was before.

But why now? Did it really matter now? And then he remembered Hallie. She was still beside him, so very still, breathing quietly as though waiting for something.

He whispered to her again, "Is it possible? Can you feel me here, Hallie?"

For a split second, her hands drifted to the keyboard again, hovering over it, almost trembling he thought, but then she withdrew them.

Whatever had been between them was gone. He could feel it. The delicate thread of connection had snapped. He'd broken it, although he truly didn't know how he'd achieved it in the first place.

"How am I going to use this stuff?" she said aloud. "It's good, but it doesn't really fit." Her hand brushed her forehead, that sensation again. And then she rubbed her temples.

Her head hurt. He knew it. Being in close proximity, he was somehow keyed into some physical sensations that she experienced. He hadn't begun to fathom the perimeters of this odd new existence of his. In fact, he suspected, he hadn't even scratched the surface.

Standing up behind her, he lightly touched each side of her head with his hands and began to massage gently. He felt her skin, the warmth radiating out from it. Even though she was oblivious to the contact, he could feel her relaxing.

Again, he asked her, "Why can't you feel me here, Hallie? I'm as real as you. I'm sure of it." But other than the unconscious response of her body to his touch, there was nothing.

And then he stopped. It was sudden, coming out of nowhere. A freezing chill quickly swept aggressively through the room. He dropped his hands from her and turned around slowly. Although it had not been moments before, the room's opposite corner was visibly darkened. He felt a shiver pass through him. There was a definite iciness coming from that direction.

"What is it? Who are you?" he spoke out instinctively. It seemed like endless minutes that he stood there waiting, and then, just as abruptly as it had manifested, he felt it withdraw.

He turned back to Hallie, and what he saw surprised him almost as much as the presence that had just vanished. She was staring into the exact corner of the room, where whatever it was had been seconds before. She knew somehow. She'd felt it, too. For the first time since he had arrived in the old house, he felt a tangible danger — a worry, not for himself but for her.

CHAPTER TWO

Great Aunt Marie

He paced. She had gone to bed hours ago, and he paced up and down the den. He retraced what he knew, turned it over in his mind, examining it from every possible angle. And there was only one conclusion he could arrive at. Man was he in over his head.

There could be no doubt because, in truth, this wasn't an unfamiliar feeling for Jack. There had been moments like this in the past, amid a crucial business negotiation for a client, when he had known it, felt it in his bones. And he'd drawn himself out of his own sense of doom and had persevered, had risen above the fray. Had, in effect, bullshitted his ass out of trouble.

He was good at that, saving his own backend. But here, now, in this setting, he didn't know the game plan, couldn't find the loopholes, backdoors. There was no one to listen to his fast talking.

There was just him and his thoughts ricocheting around in his head — just him drowning in his ignorance.

"It's not so easy, is it?"

He'd heard it — a voice, a woman's voice, but it definitely wasn't Hallie's. He looked around. The room was empty. Maybe he was losing it. Maybe that was it. He was just having a massive delusion. It wasn't the first time that possibility had occurred to him. In a way, it was more comforting than alternatives.

"No, I'm sorry, dear. There's no easy way to break this to you, but you have crossed over, bought the farm, as my father was fond of saying."

He turned around. Where minutes ago there had been empty space, there was now seated an elderly white-haired woman in the rocking chair near the fireplace. She smiled widely at him. "What was that again?" he managed to get out.

"Oh, I know it sounds a little overwhelming, but it's not all that bad once you get over the shock. I mean, where we are is a lot less trying than where my little Hallie is."

He frowned. Was she really whitewashing the fact that she'd told him he was dead? "Your little Hallie?"

"Yes, Hallie is my grandniece. I'm her Great Aunt Marie."

She stood up, although, in his estimation, it didn't make much difference. She couldn't have been any taller than four feet ten if that.

"Well," he cleared his throat, wondering exactly where this conversation should go now. It wasn't as if the thought hadn't occurred to him, but he'd dismissed it. Could he really feel this much alive, if he wasn't? "Great Aunt Marie, so what you're saying is that I've died?"

"Yes, not exactly what you expected, is it? It was a bit of a shock for me as well when I crossed over. It's sort of more like walking into a different room than all that eternal peace stuff."

He tried to assimilate her words for a moment. Now, how did this happen to him?

"The heart attack was terribly serious. Remember that, Jack?" It was as though she was listening to his thoughts.

"The heart attack—" He recalled the pain in his chest. It seemed so quick. Was that how it felt to have a heart attack? The whole memory was foggy, like a dream.

"Sometimes the transition can be hard, Jack. Some don't want to accept that they've made it at all."

He sank down onto Hallie's incredibly soft couch. All of this was hitting him very oddly. He should be more upset, he supposed, but it felt a bit like an unspoken truth that, well, now was spoken. "But I don't understand. Shouldn't there have been a tunnel, people waiting for me, or something. But there wasn't any of that. I just woke up here, trapped in Hallie's house. Is this my afterlife, this old farmhouse?"

Her smile dimmed a little, "Yes, well, that's just it. There's a reason all of this doesn't seem quite right." She paused as though carefully choosing her words, "Jack, I have to tell you this isn't, well, the usual protocol for these things. So, all I can piece together is that you're here for a special reason."

He waited expectantly, but she seemed content not to elaborate. "So, what you're saying is that you don't know. I thought once you've passed over everything would be clear."

"Goodness no, although wouldn't that be nice?" she chuckled in amusement. "Some things become clear, but others are as clear as mud. You must understand whether you are where we are, or even where you used to be, it's all about learning, evolving, every bit. Though most don't realize it at the time."

He stood up and walked over to the fireplace. He didn't know if he could have headaches anymore, but he felt as though he did. "This is a lot to take in."

She was behind him, lightly patting his shoulder. Although a bit frustrating, she seemed like a kind person. He sort of wished that she'd been his aunt. He could have used such a benign presence in his life. Turning back to her, "Are you trapped here too?"

"Oh no, I'm just visiting. I check in on Hallie from time to time. She's had a difficult life."

His eyes focused toward the hallway leading to her bedroom. He'd forgotten for a moment about what had happened in the study.

She nodded, "That was remarkable, Jack."

"What was?" he murmured, still wrestling with the enormity of it all.

"The contact with Hallie, that was most unusual. It takes a great deal for us to reach those still existing on the physical plane." She was nearly beaming at him, genuinely excited about his success.

"Funny, I thought I was existing on the physical plane."

She grinned at him with her sparsely wrinkled, heart-shaped face. Her eyes were the purest blue that he ever remembered seeing. "Well, Jack, I know that's how it feels now. But you are, and you're not. There are all kinds of planes of existence."

How did she seem to have a knack for making the worst news seem not nearly so bad with her cheerful disposition? She certainly would have been useful on his team — way back when.

"But still feeling connected to the world may help you in what you have to do."

He looked at her quizzically, "And that is what exactly?"

Another well-meaning smile," I don't know, but it must be important. Don't you think?"

He smiled back at her. He just couldn't help feeling her enthusiasm spread to him a bit. "I suppose. I suppose it must be."

He sat beside her bed in a small, cherry wood rocking chair. It seemed rather old, possibly an antique. Evidently, Hallie was fond of rocking chairs. He'd counted four in the house. He listened peacefully to her light breathing. Being near her did seem to have a calming effect on his well-challenged nerves.

And he had always been drawn to beauty. There was no denying that Hallie Barkly was beautiful.

It wasn't an aggressive beauty or even an obvious one but rather like a subtle painting whose dimensions of texture only become apparent upon close scrutiny. She was a person you needed to take time with. And just now, he seemed to have all the time in the world.

Her hair was one of his favorite things. It was just packed full of shades and highlights. At the moment, it lay carelessly and unevenly strewn amongst her six, well beaten down pillows.

These he'd counted twice. Indeed, there were six. He wondered vaguely how she didn't smother herself at night amongst them all.

His initial opinion of her hadn't changed that much. She certainly was, for lack of a better description, quirky — soft, perhaps gentle — but amusingly quirky. He wondered what she would think if she knew he was sitting next to her bed watching her sleep.

Jack had accepted that he was a ghost, a member of the non-real sector of society. This was incontrovertible now, but he still didn't feel it at all. He felt as he always had, like a man — a confused, lost man. In fact, right now, he was feeling like a bit of a voyeur, peering into a life in which he had not been formally invited.

He relaxed back in the chair and closed his eyes. Vaguely, he wondered what Hallie might be dreaming. And in that instant, he discovered how quickly what he thought could be translated into reality. In one blindingly rapid sweep, his curiosity drew him instantaneously to a place where he had not expected to be.

It was a room — a vast, enormous, cold room made almost entirely of stone.

He stood motionless on the panoramic threshold, frozen in shock at this turn of events.

Where in the hell could — he turned about shakily, still stunned by the utter massiveness of this new environment. It was absolutely overwhelming. It felt as though he'd fallen into another time, centuries and centuries ago.

The room was void of ornamentation, except for a few sparse arrangements of what appeared to be medieval armor and boldly colored wall tapestries. The chill of the stone walls actually seemed to be physically seeping into him, which only served to increase his mounting sense of panic.

All of this reminded him of something. It was like a sort of medieval throne room that he'd seen in an old Sinbad movie once.

"Sir Jackoryn, welcome to my domain."

The booming voice nearly jolted him into a backflip. He'd been so overcome by the surroundings that it hadn't occurred to him he wasn't alone. He whirled around in the direction of the sound. Well, naturally, he hadn't noticed. He had been addressed from across a football field of a distance.

Again, it boomed, "You may approach, Sir Jackoryn." Peering toward the source of the sound from what he could make out, it looked to be a figure seated on an elevated pedestal made of, what else, stone, on what could be nothing else than a throne.

His guess was that he approached the reigning monarch, speaking out from the seat of power of whatever bizarre realm he'd stumbled into.

What was the protocol in such instances? At a loss at how to respond, he slowly began to make his way toward the imposing figure that awaited him across the granite-like expanse.

The walk itself was tough going—absolutely sluggish. He dragged as he walked, and something tangible seemed to be weighing him down.

As he struggled to approach the kingly one, he could see that the figure was cloaked in purely white-silver battle armaments, accented by drippings of dark red cloth that peaked dramatically from beneath the armor. It was quite striking, even he had to admit.

The barbarian monarch, as he labeled him, was quite a picturesque display — a startling contrast of color against the blackest coal-colored beard and the pale white skin of his flesh.

He made a vivid image — a dark prince, a vision right out of a cheap gothic novel.

Ahhh, he halted. It dawned on him like a delicate sledgehammer, perhaps just like something out of one of Hallie's novels.

Awkwardly, he continued his trek for a closer view, simultaneously acknowledging for the first time that he clanked as he walked. He looked down. Now, why hadn't he noticed this before? Maybe because it wasn't there before!

His chest, his legs, his arms — all were armored. Also, in his newly arrived wardrobe was a tunic beneath the armor of light green cloth that protruded enough to noticeably contrast with the dark prince across the room. Now, his mind was beginning to get with the program. In this, unfortunately, predictable tableau that would cast him as, and his heart dropped perceptively, **the good guy**.

The realization gave him chills. It all fit together in a peculiar, skewed sort of way. The scene was cast. Evidently, tonight, he was playing the pure, good, boring character, and whoever the joker on the throne might be was the dark, conflicted, smoldering anti-hero. It wasn't hard to size up how heavily the deck was stacked against him. In the purest of female hearts, in particular what he had gleaned of Hallie Barkly's during his limited exposure to her, he felt intrinsically he didn't stand a snowball's chance in hell at being victorious and achieving the spoils, whatever the spoils might be.

He stopped, out of breath, still yards away from the throne. Even from where he was, he could see his eyes — his nemesis' eyes. They were a deep, sparkling, dark color. It gave his appearance an unreal, hypnotic quality. Much as he hated to admit it, there was no denying it. He was compelling. Hell, if he were a woman, he'd throw his hat in with this guy.

"Sir Jackoryn," boomed the deep but velvety voice.

He looked around for a moment and then asked pointedly. "Is that really my name?"

The dark prince smiled widely enough that his perfectly shaped, uncannily white teeth presented themselves. "Well, you must admit Sir Jack wouldn't quite fit the motif. And, after all, I am not its author."

"Yes, well speaking of that, where is the fair damsel?"

And as if on cue, she suddenly appeared on the threshold of the great medieval throne room that Jack concluded had been borne out of her imagination. It was Hallie, but not the Hallie as Jack had seen her. Here, she was not that odd, quirky, unpredictable woman he'd been coming to know. Here, she was transfigured, draped in a shimmering gown made entirely of golden cloth. Her skin was absolutely luminescent against its luster. And her hair, drawn up loosely by jeweled combs, cascaded with escaping golden ringlets framing her perfectly creamy skin and dark pink mouth until all he could utter was, "Wow."

"Does Sir Jackoryn approve?" The male counterpart to her loveliness inquired from the throne.

"Would you please stop calling me that." He snapped with irritation. He didn't want intrusion right now. He was still drinking deeply from the vision of Hallie. His mind was calculating furiously at lightning speed. There had to be a way for him to turn this around and get the girl, just had to be.

Hallie floated toward him, her mouth trembling with the fullness and intensity of her thoughts, or so he guessed.

"Jackoryn, I did not know you would be here."

He smiled. This was novel. Here, they were actually speaking, instead of her just looking right through him. "That makes two of us."

"I know you can't understand, but I must stay here with Samory."

"Ah, so this is Samory?"

"You mustn't be so jocular with my heart."

"I'm sorry. I didn't realize I was doing that, uh Lady Hallie."

"Hallea."

"Of course, right, Lady Hallea, can we take just a moment or so to talk about this? Don't you owe me that much?" The guilt card was always helpful. "Honestly, this guy over here, I can tell you right now, you have no future with. It's written all over him."

She frowned, seemingly a little befuddled by his responses.

Perhaps he was not following the script. "There is nothing to say, Jackoryn. You have lost," the anti-hero boomed behind him.

He turned to the overconfident monarch. "Look, big guy. I walked in during the middle of this. But I'm here now and not ready to give up before I've started." And then, he added, "You might want to check that anemia, pal. You look like you're one foot in the grave already."

Small, cold hands gripped his arms, "Please, Jackoryn, you tear my heart out. I must stay with Samory. I must try and save him."

He stopped for a second and looked deeply into her eyes. It was there — that same soft, vulnerable look that had as of late become so familiar to him. There was no doubt she had created this. But he also saw something else that disturbed him — the fringes of panic in her expression. She was in trouble here. She needed him. Something was smoldering, brewing beneath all the finery of this illusion. Hallie seemed extremely ill at ease, and why should she be? After all, wasn't this her ball game?

He returned her gentle embrace, holding the sides of her arms gently. "Hallie, Hallie," he whispered, "listen to me. Let me take you out of here. I bet I have a nice white stallion outside just waiting for the two of us."

Her eyes narrowed a bit, "You jest, Jackoryn."

"Well, if not, then we can walk, but I can't leave you here like this, not with him."

"But he is my destiny. I am here to save him."

"Maybe, maybe not, maybe it isn't him you're supposed to save. Maybe it's me."

An eyebrow lifted, "You?"

"Yes, me, my life hasn't been too wonderful, and you have to admit that I don't come quite with the baggage that guy seems to have."

"Enough, Jackoryn, leave now, or I will have you flayed," Samory boomed.

She pulled away, "You must go, Jackoryn. It isn't safe for you here."

He grasped a small delicate hand. It felt so cold. Why did she feel like ice here? "Hallie, I have a strong feeling it isn't safe for you either. Let me help you."

And then, for a split second, something shifted. He felt it, just like what had happened for only seconds in the study. An odd recognition swept across her features, and her soft brown eyes widened.

And then, he was back, next to her bed. She was awake, sitting up, just staring forward. "Hallie," he whispered again.

But there was no response this time, none at all.

She flung open the door, declaring, "We're home!" The long black puppy she held in her arms seemed to markedly tremble at her enthusiasm. That certainly wasn't a good sign. Hallie had left his cage in the car, wanting her new charge to experience its home with full sensory advantage. But upon entering, it just turned its cold black nose back to her and tried to nuzzle in closer.

She had picked out the orphan at the SPCA. It wasn't something she'd planned to do, but then again, she was a spontaneous kind of person. In truth, she had to admit, the impulse had been seeded when she'd first awoken that morning. Something odd had come over her — a peculiar feeling. Hallie experienced an emotion that was really unfamiliar to her. For the first time since she had moved into the old Virginia farmhouse, she felt lonely. By nature, she was a solitary individual, a loner of sorts, so being by herself had never posed a problem. But today, the emotion had hit her hard. It had nagged at her all through the early morning hours. She felt bereft of, well, companionship.

This was actually truly unique. Even when she had been married to Edward, she didn't feel lonely when he was gone. They were too distant and too different to truly connect or feel the other's absence.

This was silly. She told herself. There was no rational reason for feeling this. But she was experiencing a tangible sensation of loss, almost as though she had found something and then lost it again. But all of that was ludicrous because absolutely nothing had changed since yesterday.

Maybe Monica was right. She was just spending way too much time in her own imagination.

So, she dressed and went out for a drive, passing a sign for the local SPCA, and the rest was history.

Of course, things would change now. When she left here, she'd have to find an apartment or place that would take pets.

But then maybe she would buy her own house with a yard. She certainly had saved enough money from Sebastian Winter's book sales.

Ouch, even the thought of the book brought her pain. It wasn't going well, not at all. Instead of an easy flow of words, it was as though each thought was becoming a labor to get onto the page. It would be so easy just to fall back onto the familiar pattern of horror that Sebastian Winters had been known to produce, but she truly wanted to write something different this time — a tale of redemption. It was an undertaking that was becoming more arduous than she had first imagined.

Hopefully, the new addition to the household would generate inspiration. At the very least, he would be a distraction. She looked down at the trembling little piece of existence that had not moved an inch from the spot where she had placed it. As she picked him up, he looked at her with wide, dark eyes. "What am I going to do with you? How about breakfast while we think of a name to call you?" He nuzzled her with the now moist, cold, black nose. "I suppose that's as much an answer as I'm going to get." And she headed into the kitchen with her new companion. "You're going to like it here Samson. No, that doesn't quite do it, does it?"

Monica nudged Hallie's new puppy away from the black leather bag that he seemed intent on chewing up. "Hallie, what on earth possessed you to get this thing? All it seems to want to do is eat everything."

"No, he's teething. He's only three months old — just a baby."

"Couldn't you get something that was already trained? Shew, you mongrel." She nudged it away with the toe of her black leather pump, which it now seemed intent on nibbling as well. "Do you have any idea how much these shoes cost me?"

Aunt Marie frowned at Monica. She and Jack stood across the room near the fireplace, watching the exchange. "You know, I never understood why she remained friends with that girl. They're nothing alike."

"Maybe that's the attraction."

"Yes, well, that's something a man would say."

"Well, I—"

"You know Edward was the same way, so very different from her." She cut him off abruptly. He'd noticed Hallie's short, white-haired aunt had a habit of doing that when she wasn't interested in what he had to say. "They had very little in common, but he was the one she had to have."

"Maybe she was looking for something she felt lacking in herself."

She looked at him with her uncompromising blue eyes. "Is that what you used to do, Jack?"

Monica continued grumpily, "You know I've heard the better pet shops have already started training the dogs before you even buy them. What kind did you say this was?"

"He's a mix, a mutt. I got him from the SPCA."

She flung back her blond hair in exasperation, "You know that's like going to the Salvation Army for your clothes."

Hallie walked over and picked him up, "I think he's beautiful." And she smiled with adoration as he began biting her index finger in earnest. "And I hear you can find some very interesting things at the Salvation Army."

"You are hopeless."

"And you're a snob. But I won't hold it against you. Not yet, anyway."

"So, what are you calling it?"

Hallie frowned as she tried to wrench her finger free. "I haven't decided."

Monica leaned back with distaste and crossed her legs, which were well exposed by a slit in her snugly fitted skirt. Hallie had decided long ago that she must have a closet full of these.

"So why don't you call him Sebastian?"

"I thought of that, but it doesn't seem to fit. He's not a snooty sort of dog. I want a more, well, normal type name."

"What, like Spot?"

"No." Hallie continued to pet his head. She'd really become attached to him in the week they'd been together. And his initial shock of being here had dissipated quickly, as her chewed-on furniture could testify to. "Actually, I like the name Jack."

From across the room, Jack's eyebrow peaked at the mention of his name. Great Aunt Marie smiled at him with a knowing expression on her cherubic face. "And you didn't think you were making any progress."

"Jack?" Monica quibbled, "That's well, so boring."

"She's got to go," he whispered adamantly to Aunt Marie.

"I don't think it's boring," Hallie declared enthusiastically. "I think it suits him. Besides, you don't like it, so I must be on to something."

Monica sighed with feigned exasperation, "Oh, fine. You're going to do what you want to anyway. But I did come here to talk to you about something. I went ahead and made some arrangements. And before you protest, you should know it's for your own good."

Hallie frowned, "When anyone ever says for my own good, I can't help but anticipate catastrophe."

She leaned in closer to her friend, her cool brown eyes sparkling for the first time since Jack had seen her. "Oh, don't be negative. I've arranged a date for you."

There was a vacuous moment of stunned silence. "You're not serious."

"Well, it would be kind of a double date. It's a guy who works at my office. I told him all about you, about you being an author, and he is very enthusiastic."

"He knows my work?"

"Well, he knows that you're an author. Come on, just dinner tomorrow night in Richmond. You can spend the night at my place."

"Look, Monica, I guess you mean well. I guess you do," she repeated without conviction. "But I just—"

"Please, Hallie, as a personal favor to me. I've already told him you'd be there, and I'll look bad if you don't show."

"You know you are ruthless. I'm really afraid this is a mistake."

"Come on Hal, say yes."

"Well, what about Jack?"

"Leave his food out. Jack can rough it for one night."

Hallie sighed, reluctant to resist further. "All right, but I've got to tell you, I don't hold out much hope for this going well."

"Don't be so pessimistic. You must be open to new experiences."

Jack felt disgruntled. He didn't trust this, didn't trust Monica as far as he could throw her, and in his present state, that wasn't far at all. "Well, she's wrong about one thing."

"What's that?" Aunt Marie asked with evident interest.

"Jack is definitely going along. At least this Jack is."

CHAPTER THREE

Jacob McFarin

His namesake had been following him around ever since Monica left. Almost from the day Hallie first brought the puppy home, Jack realized the dog could see him. The little black mutt had been tentative at first. It had been tentative about everything at first. But Jack had seen its eyes fix directly on him across the room. He had even barked at him — initially, perhaps not knowing what Jack's presence in Hallie's house meant, but, then again, he certainly wasn't alone in that regard. Maybe Jack Jr., as he was apt to call him, instinctually felt the difference between him and Hallie. Or maybe he was just another person to the dog.

To just be another person and not exist in this between state was a refreshing idea. The frustration inside him was overwhelming at times. It was extremely irritating that he felt so ineffectual in Hallie's world. But even beyond that, there was a growing awareness that there was something else, some other kind of living beyond Hallie's farmhouse, that he needed to get on with. An insidious tug-of-war was starting to play out inside of him — an emerging struggle between the desire to leave and the desire to somehow finish whatever he was meant to do here. He wondered, ultimately, what would win out.

However, it was clear that Hallie noticed the dog's odd behavior. He could see it. From time to time, she would stop what she was doing and follow the direction of Jack Jr.'s gaze right to him. Then she would frown, evidently seeing nothing where he stood. It would make him frown, too. He didn't like being this sort of non-person where she was concerned. In a way, he was growing quite possessive of her, sort of in a big brother type of way and sort of not. It was an interesting cocktail of emotions he didn't want to look at too closely. If he ever sorted them all out, what good would it do?

He couldn't do anything about it, could he? Paramount, beyond all this mishmash of introspection on his part, he knew one thing — clear as crystal. He didn't want Hallie on a date with some clown that Monica Quimby had picked out.

"What do you think of this one, Jack?" Hallie called from the bedroom. Jack indulgently pretended at times that she was talking to him and even verbalized an answer like, "I don't know, honey. Why don't you come out and show me?" But as she flew out of the bedroom in a different garment, he knew it was the dog she wanted a response from.

Jack Jr. sat curled up at his feet as they both waited for Hallie to model her potential outfits for the big night. Out of respect, he had stayed out of the bedroom while she was changing, and the dog, out of lack of interest, had done so, too.

She came sauntering into the room wearing a flowing red sundress that Jack had to admit was truly fetching and, thus, potentially dangerous. She swirled around, "What do you think, Jack? I bought this one right after the divorce with Edward. I was hoping to wear it to his funeral," she smiled, sheepishly giggling. "Just kidding." But Jack suspected that she wasn't, not completely. "So, anyway, what do you think?"

The dog lifted his head and looked up at Jack, as had been his practice with every other potential outfit. Jack put out his thumb and turned it down with the dramatic flair of a Roman emperor. The dog turned its head back to Hallie and gave his most disgusted growl. They truly made a good team.

"Are you serious? You don't like this one either. I really don't have that much left to choose from." She looked genuinely distraught as she headed for the bedroom, but Jack had to wonder about a woman who let a dog pick out her clothes.

If he had his way, she would go to Richmond wearing something akin to a nun's garb. No need to impress those who weren't likely to appreciate her. "All right, Jack, I just don't have anything else, so one of these will have to do. If you're going to help me, come on."

He bent down and whispered into Jack Jr.'s furry ear. "Just make sure she doesn't wear the red dress." The little black dog looked into his eyes as if to say his mission was understood, then disappeared into the bedroom.

Jack leaned back in the chair remembering Hallie in the red dress, her cheeks blooming with color, and then the Hallie of the dream draped in the golden gown. It was more than the fact that he was stuck in this house with no one to look at but her. Things had gone way beyond that here. He was looking at her too close. Getting to know her unguarded moments that others would never see — and being fascinated by them. She was like a puzzle to him or one of those cube games that he couldn't quite get the solution right — frustrating, yes, but intensely fascinating.

Foolish man, foolish dead man to let his thoughts wander in pointless directions. He pulled his attention to the matter at hand — the disagreeable thought of her dating someone. Well, suffice it to say that no one Monica Quimby could produce had a right to her. That was the excuse he used, and it was sound enough to almost convince himself.

The margarita had a strong sour taste and abundant salt around the edges of the rather substantial green-tinted glass. At least that was good. She hated the kind that was too sweet.

She remembered Edward not being able to handle a margarita that was too sour. It was a strange contradiction in his personality. His demeanor and cutting sarcasm were so bitingly acidic, yet he liked his margaritas sweet. In fact, oftentimes, he would end up getting some fruity variety, like strawberry or peach. Hallie had always found that very comical about him and very telling.

"Hey, Hallie, what do you think of the place?"

"What?" Her mind was drawn back to the oddly animated face of Monica Quimby. It had become evident to her that Monica had been on a mission all night. She was bound and determined that the group of four seated amid a Friday night crowd at La Casa Grande should have fun, even if she had to manually force the joy down all of their respective throats.

"The restaurant, the margarita, Greg here, you're not giving any of them much attention."

Hallie smiled back at the joyful Monica, whose slitted brown eyes darted little sparks of rage in her direction. "Oh, I'm sorry. My mind wandered. The place is, well, very atmospheric."

The younger man seated next to her cleared his throat, "Well, that should appeal to your writer's imagination, right Hallie?" She turned to him and smiled blandly. His teeth were perfect sheets of white peering from behind thin lips. He seemed nice enough, nice looking, curly brown hair, but obviously a good five to ten years her junior. What the hell was Monica thinking? "Um, what sorts of books do you write, Hallie? Monica said something about political thrillers."

She deliberately took a big slurp of her sour margarita, "No, not exactly."

Monica beamed with calculation, "Well, they do have a lot of mystery in them, right Hal."

"They're vampire books."

The two yuppie gentlemen turned with surprise at the announcement. Richard Belkin, Monica's date for the evening, reflected the most genuine expression of vacuous astonishment that Hallie could ever remember witnessing. "Really? Well, that's not what you said—"

Monica compulsively jumped in, "Well, they do have a political spin, you know — metaphorically socially relevant and all of that."

Richard, a contained business type, seemingly well-groomed but with closely cropped red hair of an amazingly bright shade, was not to be sidelined by her friend's subterfuge. To Hallie, he inquired pointedly, "Is this true, Hallie? Do you write with a politically metaphorical intent?"

She looked at him and smiled with a humor that seemed to draw its strength from her margarita glass. She also wondered what the hell he'd just said, "No, Richard, I don't."

There was a delightful splash of stunned silence, and then the youngish Greg, who seemed intent on protecting her for some obscure reason that she didn't want to fathom, interjected, "Well, Hallie, then what do your books mean?"

She picked up an oversized chip and dipped it in the salsa sauce that seemed determined to scorch her lips. Although, at the moment, she was curiously numb to it. "They don't mean anything. They're about a vampire that kills people."

He was smiling, but she couldn't see his overly bright teeth anymore. "Really?"

She was truly beginning to feel bubbly now, "You know, I do like this restaurant, Monica. What a great choice. I hope dinner comes soon. I'm starving."

Monica's glinting eyes seemed frozen in her face now, "Well, Richard, tell us about that new project you've been working on."

His mouth pinched a little as he took a not too effective stab at sarcasm. "Oh, I doubt that would sound too interesting after hearing about Hallie's vampire books," he sniped.

Hallie noted the pained expression on Monica's face. This Richard was beginning to remind her of Edward a bit. Of course, she'd always thought that Monica and Edward would have been a better match. Honestly, though, she'd never met anyone she thought would be a good match for her. Sighing, she ate another big chip.

Their portly Mexican waiter, still wearing an oversized green sombrero, approached the table; "Your food is on its way. Can I get anything else for you amigos?"

Hallie piped up cheerfully, "Yes, another Margarita."

Monica added glumly, "How about another round for everyone?"

He watched and that depressed him. He missed the flesh — moving among people, smoking a cigarette, having a drink, and putting his arms around a beautiful woman. And Hallie, his Hallie, she was hilarious tonight. Hallie was drunk, but she was dazzling. He actually felt a little sorry for the inept young man that Monica had chosen for her. He was obviously way over his head, trying to make some sort of connection with the moody and mysterious brunette. But she had shut him down immediately, and for Jack, that brought a further admiration for the woman who was increasingly becoming so pivotal in his transient existence.

Monica, of course, had chosen wrong. That in itself wasn't a huge surprise. She hadn't impressed him with any depth of perception. She wasn't really capable of seeing the quick mind and soft beauty of Hallie Barkly, for who he had a growing appreciation. It was too subtle for her kind and admittedly, not to his credit, he hadn't seen it right away himself. He had once, not so long ago, spent the balance of his time mixing amongst that superficial breed, but not now. Something integral had shifted in him or, rather, had been awakened. He felt that somehow, he'd always been different, misplaced, but just elected to ignore it.

But here, when it was really too late for him, he was beginning to want more.

Being around her, knowing who she was and what he couldn't have, was quietly torturing him.

It hadn't been a late evening. Monica's date seemed intent on cutting things short. "You know you could have tried a little harder. Did you even let Greg kiss you goodnight?"

"I was kind of waiting for him to grow hair on his face before we made out."

"He's not that young," she sniped back.

Hallie's head was pounding. She buried it in a pillow on Monica's couch. "Please, he's a schoolboy."

"All right, I admit it. I thought you might do better with someone who wouldn't be in control of things. And it would have been all right if you hadn't drunk so much."

"It was the only thing that kept me from bolting out the door."

"You know, I'm going to have to smooth all of this over with Richard."

"Richard is a prick," she retorted with emphasis.

"He is not. He just has high standards."

"And things would have gone so much better if I had just written political thrillers."

"You know, I'm trying to help you, trying to keep you from burying yourself in that house." Monica fired back. Jack marveled at their exchange, wondering what on earth tied this relationship together. It was so odd to sit back and watch the fireworks. Monica doggedly clung to her pose of being a caring friend, but it was completely superficial or confused at best.

He'd settled on the deep burgundy brocade couch in Monica's Condo. Hallie had curled up on the other end, retreating into a pained little lump.

"Maybe I like being buried," she groaned. "I certainly prefer it to evenings like this one."

Monica flung her blond head in exasperation. "Fine, I won't make the mistake of trying to help you again."

"Is that a promise?" She grumpily retorted. It was the liquor that had loosened her tongue. He wondered if, indeed, their peculiar affinity would survive the aftermath of this brutal honesty, not really caring if it didn't.

"You know, if it were up to you Edward would be the last man you ever had anything to do with."

"Would that be such a tragedy?"

Monica just stood hovering near the couch, her brown eyes reflecting something else. Maybe she did care in her own bizarre fashion. "I don't know Hallie. Is he the last man you ever want to love?"

"I don't want to love anyone tonight. I just want this night to end." Her voice was muffled. She was talking straight into her pillow.

"You know, you certainly get bitchy after you drink too much."

"As opposed to being that way all the time."

"I'll ignore that. Do you want some sheets for the couch?"

"No, just go away so my head will stop hurting."

"All right, we'll talk about this in the morning." She went off in a huff — the door to Monica's bedroom closing in something between a shut and a slam. Whatever it was really hurt Hallie's head. This was ridiculous. Weren't hangovers supposed to occur the next morning? Maybe she was just cursed.

She kicked off her black leather pumps and pulled the dark green throw from Monica's couch up to her chin. She didn't even have the energy to change from the black halter dress she'd chosen for the evening. Maybe if she'd worn the red, all would have been different. Maybe if she were different, all would be different. She thought about Jack and wondered if he was all right, if he had eaten all the food she'd left out, if he was sleeping on her bed tonight.

Jack leaned over her and touched her hair as she fell asleep. It felt warm to his fingertips. As she drifted off, she murmured something inaudible. He indulged himself and thought that in this between state she could feel him near her.

"Goodnight, Hallie. Sweet dreams."

He smiled to himself. Perhaps it wasn't right, but he was feeling very territorial with her. Admittedly, he'd been jealous and was well pleased with the night's outcome, except the part of her never loving another man. She had too much to give. That just couldn't be right.

Gabriella was torn in her heart, caught between a place of shadows and of light. She knelt upon one of the soft velvet pews of St. Michel's Cathedral and prayed in reverence for the almighty to guide her out of her torment. Her spirit clung to what was good and right, but her heart was traitorous. It had been drawn into the twisted web of darkness that was Samory's existence. Tears flooded from her soft brown eyes, her soul enmeshed torturously in the confusion and betrayal of her very essence. How could she truly love one such as he?

As she bent her head in heartfelt agony, behind her, she heard the heavy drop of footsteps begin the long walk down the marble aisle at the heart of St. Michel's. Unexpectedly startled, her heart clutched in surprise as the sound ceased abruptly just beside her. She lifted her tear-filled eyes hesitantly, only to see a stranger staring down at her.

Hallie paused for a moment, stuck. She was completely stalled. Really, it was kind of nuts adding another character to the mix just now. It certainly hadn't been her original plan. Actually, the idea had popped into her head on her drive home from Richmond, and then increasingly had been nagging at her all day.

She had left Monica's early, neither in the mood nor the proper physical state to entertain any rehashing of the night before. But she had inferred from her friend's aloof behavior at their brief parting that Monica was none too eager to prolong her stay. She evidently had more serious concerns, namely smoothing the water with old carrot-top Richard. It was just as well. Hallie was out of sorts and suddenly preoccupied with a piece she felt was missing from her book. There needed to be more struggle, sort of like—

"A triangle, a love triangle," Jack spoke it out loud for what felt like the thousandth time that day. It had occurred to him during the night that the easiest and best way to connect with

Hallie was through her writing, and what better way than to introduce himself as—

He was a tall man, a tall, muscular man whose face was well-tanned. It was evident, even to Gabriella, in her state of upset, that he had spent much of his time outdoors amongst the elements. His hair was a light brown, nearly of a chestnut shade, as was the well-clipped beard on his face. But it was his eyes that were astonishing. They were not like the dark obsidian pools of Samory but rather a deep blue hue, clear and vibrant like the living ocean. She smiled involuntarily as something distant and almost unfamiliar coursed through her veins — the sudden, sweet, desperate rush of hope.

And then she stopped. Hallie's hands froze, paralyzed over the keyboard. Something had gripped her like a vise descending — a crushing, sudden feeling of panic and confusion targeted around her heart area. She sat, breathing shallowly, feeling completely stunned. Jack felt it, too. It was obvious that something was violently resisting this. He sensed the tangible blast of iciness directed toward Hallie. Scanning the room, he again could perceive nothing visual.

"Where the hell are you, you coward?" He demanded angrily. But there was no response, only the persistent, relentless cold.

Then, as though something was guiding him, an idea crossed his mind. He tried to mentally picture Hallie surrounded by a blanket of warm air blocking the chill that had come into the room. He focused intensely, with all his concentration on the image. Beside him, he could hear her breathing deeply.

"Okay, take it easy," he whispered.

Several times, her fingers reached out to touch the keyboard, and then she withdrew. He bent in close to her and spoke softly in her ear. "It's all right. She looks into his deep blue eyes."

She nodded as if to reassure herself and then started typing.

"I'm sorry, sir. You look as though you recognize me from somewhere."

He smiled in an enigmatic fashion that made Gabriella exceedingly uncomfortable. "I must admit that I have come a long way to find you, Mademoiselle. You are undoubtedly Gabriella Martresse."

She stood up, self-consciously straightening out her long, satiny skirt that had been crushed momentarily while she was kneeling. "I am sorry, sir. You have me at a disadvantage. You know who I am, but I have no idea who you are."

The stranger smiled widely with a curious glint in his eyes that almost made her blush under the scrutiny of his gaze. "Forgive me, my lady. I am the captain of a seafaring vessel that has originated from the ports of the Americas. My name is Jacob, Jacob McFarin and, if I may speak bluntly, I am here to rescue you."

The little black dog followed Hallie around the house in a state of what Jack could only perceive as bewilderment. She would move from one room to another with what seemed to be deliberate purpose and then leave off, drifting away in thought, absently passing by the love-starved pup. Jack Jr. had several times wandered near him in a state of confusion. He didn't understand, as Jack did, that his owner was preoccupied, caught in another world of her own making.

She had only written a brief introduction of Jacob Mcfarin's character, but even that seemed to bother her. At first, he thought perhaps it was the struggle that had taken place with the unknown entity, but the expressions reflecting on her face were not of upset or concern.

Once in a while, he could detect the slightest flicker of a smile. If she were another woman, he would have said she had just met someone new, someone who interested her — perhaps even attracted her.

When she finally settled in one spot for a while, she curled up on the recliner in the den holding a delicate heart-shaped necklace in her hand she had picked up in the bedroom. It was one he hadn't seen her with before. He stood across from her, silently focusing in on her eyes. They had a faraway look that leaped out at him. It was actually physically tormenting, at least as physical as he could be. Jack knew women, and he knew that Hallie was daydreaming. And if he didn't miss the mark, she was daydreaming with interest about the seafarer Jacob McFarin. Damn the bastard, it was a hell of a position to be in, to be jealous of your own self-created character. What was all of this? He wanted, well damn it, what he wanted right now wasn't possible, but that certainly didn't stop him from wanting it.

"Well, Mr. Jacob McFarin, I presume."

Jack turned to the round face of Hallie's great Aunt Marie, "Don't rub it in."

"No, no, it seems like a good move to me, my boy. You, well, he, seems to have reached her in a fashion."

He took a deep breath, trying to focus. "Yes, but what's my next move?" Hallie continued to hold the necklace in her hand, unconsciously fingering it absently almost as though she were meditating with rosary beads. "Where did the necklace come from?"

"I gave it to her on her sixteenth birthday. She carries it around when she is particularly bothered about something. That's why I'm here. I could feel her thinking about me."

"You can actually feel when someone thinks about you?"

She smiled, "What are you feeling, Jack?"

"Like I'm ready to jump out of my skin if I had any to jump out of. I'm feeling—" his eyes focused on Hallie again. Her expression was intense, as though she was trying to visualize something. "I feel this pull, this tremendous pull to her."

She nodded, "She's reaching out to you."

"How can that be? She doesn't know I exist."

"Her mind doesn't know it, but you've struck a chord in her. Truth always bypasses what the conscious mind perceives as truth."

He looked at her with confusion. "You want to run that one by me again?"

Smiling indulgently, "Not especially."

And then he remembered the episode in the study. "There is something I'm worried about. I keep sensing something else here, some sort of presence, though I haven't actually seen it. And from what I gather, it doesn't like me much."

"That can't be too much of a new experience for you, Jack," she giggled. "Seriously though, I know what you're talking about, but for some reason, I am blocked from helping you."

"Blocked?"

"Seems so. Things work a little differently where we are, Jack. It's all about learning, and nothing can interfere with that." She stopped.

"And?" He waited for her to elaborate.

She was focused on Hallie again. "And, I think you should stay close to her, Jack. Stay very close."

He nodded, his eyes lingering on Hallie's soft expression. Yes, he would stay close. That was exactly what he intended to do.

CHAPTER FOUR

Gabriella

She didn't dream that night. She just tossed and turned, waking up constantly to look at the clock. It was about two in the morning when Hallie surrendered. She gave up on sleeping and instead made herself a cup of peppermint tea. The study beckoned her. She needed to write more, needed it almost like a physical torment, but a part of her resisted. Perhaps it was just obstinance.

It bothered her immensely — this new presence in the narrative, Captain Jacob McFarin. And there was no real reason that it should. Hadn't it been her choice to bring him into the mix? Hadn't it?

Then why did he bug her so much? He wasn't a vampire like Samory. But there was a comfort in Samory. She knew what he was, knew him inside and out, but this new man. He was the unknown and, thus, oddly more dangerous.

She allowed him to lead her down the ageless steps of the French cathedral. "Forgive me, sir, but my father is expecting me home very soon. We have a house on the outskirts of Paris."

"Then, Mademoiselle, if you would allow me, I will take you there in my carriage and perhaps converse with your father concerning your relationship with Monsieur Samory Delacroix."

She halted on the steps. Her heart clutched in fear at the discovery. "What do you mean, sir?"

"Am I to take it that your father is not aware of the perilous path that you have chosen to take with this creature?"

Gabriella's frightened eyes widened. "No, my father does not know of my engagement to Monsieur Delacroix."

"Engagement? Have things progressed that far?"

"Surely, you cannot expect me to share such private details of my life with a virtual stranger."

Jacob turned away momentarily as if to calm himself, then returned his steady and unflinching gaze to Gabriella. "My Lady, you are correct in that we are indeed strangers. Yet, I must tell you with the deepest conviction that I am well acquainted with the true nature of Monsieur Delacroix."

Her heart chilled at his declaration. "True nature? What can you mean by that?" Abruptly and most forcefully, he grasped both of her delicate hands with his large, strong, manly—

Hallie paused for a moment and leaned back in the chair. This was beginning to get a little out of hand. She took a sip of her peppermint tea but could feel her own heart racing. Beside her, Jack smiled and bent to kiss the top of her head. "Go on,

Hallie. Her small delicate hands were grasped in large, powerful ones whose strength she could feel course through her at the moment of contact."

"Gabriella," he used her first name as though it was his right to do so, although she had not given him permission. "I have traveled across the world hunting your fiancé with every ounce of relentless spirit that I could muster."

"Why?" she whispered. She tried to break free of his powerful grasp, but it was clear that he was not yet ready to release her.

"I will tell you why. Only five years ago, that monster took the innocence and then the life of my sister Margaret."

"No," the word flew out of her mouth in a gasp.

He pulled her closer, so close that she could feel the vibrant and compelling warmth of his body. He was not cold like Samory but alive, oh so alive. "It's true, Gabriella, and he will do the same to you if I allow it to happen."

Summoning all of her delicate strength, she finally wrenched herself free from his embrace. "No, you're wrong. Samory loves me. He would never hurt me."

"He might not mean to hurt you, but his murderous nature will win out."

"Jacob, you're wrong. I can save him. I know I can."

His warm blue eyes hardened at her pronouncement. "Margaret thought the same. And I was too late to save her."

She turned away from him, caught up in her own despair. But once again, she felt his powerful hands on her. This time, they slipped around her waist and then gently but deliberately pulled her back against him. He whispered in her ear, "Gabriella, I can be a ruthless man also. I am determined to save you with or without your cooperation. Inform your father that there will be a guest for dinner tonight. Do so, Mademoiselle, or I will promptly inform him of all your most recent activities."

And then he bent his head even closer and lightly brushed his lips against her cheek.

A loud crash resounded throughout the room, shattering the quiet. A standing lamp near the doorway had abruptly fallen to the floor for no apparent reason. Hallie stared at it in shock. She had nearly jumped out of her chair at the computer desk. Still trembling from the jolt, she stood up shakily. "Damn it, that scared the crap out of me."

Reluctantly, she gingerly tiptoed over to the sight of the catastrophe. The damage was substantial, considering that the light apparently had fallen with some force onto the hardwood floor. Jack watched sternly as Hallie headed down the hall to get a broom and dustpan to clean up the debris.

He stood alone, staring at the broken glass. He could still feel the irritating rush of negative energy it had taken to bring the lamp down. "Don't like where things are going, pal?" he said smugly. "Well, I've got to tell you. This is just the beginning."

Hallie stalked around the house, straightening up with a degree of contempt. She was expecting a visitor. It had been about seven 'o'clock in the morning when the phone rang. Actually, it had been only several hours before that she had finally gotten to sleep.

The first series of rings she had let the voice mail pick up, and then whoever it was called back and back and back until finally she— "Yeah, what?" she managed to get out, trying to smother her colossal irritation.

"Hallie?"

"Yes," she sat up in bed, rubbing her aching, tired eyes.

"I bet you don't know who this is."

She stared at the cell phone, seriously debating whether or not to hang up immediately. "You'd win," she snapped out more harshly than she imagined was appropriate.

Undaunted, the caller continued, "Think back now. Isn't my voice familiar?"

Her eyes widened with malice. Who the hell? "Look, whoever this is—"

"Okay, I'll give you a hint. Mexican food and lots of margaritas."

She said nothing.

"Okay, if you give up—"

"I do," with quiet steel.

"It's Greg Wasserstrom."

And then confusion, "Who?"

"Oh, come on, you're hurting my ego. You remember dinner with Dick and Monica."

She swallowed, couldn't be. "Was that really your name, Wasserstrom?"

"You're hurting my feelings."

"Look, Greg, it's kind of early for me. I was up late last night."

"Not another wild party."

"I was writing," she stated flatly and a tad perturbed.

"Yeah, that's right. Well, I just wanted to tell you that this is your lucky day." Evidently, he was not one for subtlety.

"No kidding," she murmured in a yawn.

"I'm on my way into town on business and wanted to come see you."

Again, she said nothing. She tried to dig deep into her sluggish mind for an excuse, but it was unfairly just way too early to be creative. "Um, well, Greg, I am kind of involved in doing a lot of work on the book."

"Then, you need a break."

"Ummm."

"I'll be over there about ten. I'll bring some donuts. So, don't have breakfast, just put on coffee. What's your favorite kind?"

"Kind?" Was this really happening?

"Of donut."

"Chocolate frosted." It wasn't, but nothing else came to mind.

"With sprinkles?"

"No, I don't like sprinkles." Had she snapped at him about sprinkles? She couldn't be sure.

"Super, I'll see you there. Monica gave me directions to your house so I can find you easily."

"Oh good." And then, mercifully, it all ended.

She checked around the den critically. It looked Okay. It wasn't like she wanted to impress him. It wasn't even like she wanted him here. This just felt so much like Monica. She would have to murder her later.

The doorbell rang, and she opened the door to the disturbingly white smile of Greg Wasserstrom. There seemed to be an endless stretch of awkwardness in which they just stared at each other. "Are you going to let me in, or are we going to eat donuts on the porch?" Good grief, he was chipper.

She smiled and stepped back to let him in. This was going to be rough. She didn't remember him being so annoying. But then again, she didn't remember a whole heck of a lot from that night. "Well, Hallie, this is a cozy house. Atmospheric, I guess that's good for a writer."

"It suits me. You want a plate? I mean, do you like your donuts on a plate?"

"That would be super."

She nodded, "Why don't you come in the kitchen and get your coffee?"

She waited, and then he added expectedly, "Super."

They sat at the small dinette table Hallie had placed in the breakfast nook of her kitchen. It was right next to a large window overlooking the rolling hills of her backyard. She found herself looking out of it often and wondering when Greg Wasserstrom was going to leave. It had been only about half an hour, but it had felt like a decade.

"How's your donut, Hallie? You've barely touched it."

She smiled, "Oh, my stomach is a little out of sorts today. It might be a bug," then she added, "I hope it's not contagious."

"I have to say, Hallie. After the way we connected at dinner the other night, I was glad I had this opportunity to come see you." Her eyebrow rose. Connected? Were they at the same meal? For the fourth time, Hallie heard a growl under the table.

Jack was at it again, determined to rip a hole in Greg's pants leg.

He grimaced, "Feisty little thing. Can't you lock him up or something?"

"No, he's just a puppy. He doesn't like to be alone."

Across the room, Jack was squatting down, encouraging Jack Jr. "Go on, boy, go on, harass the hell out of him."

Hallie stared at the puppy with amusement. He was usually much more intimidated by strange men. The other day, when the cable guy came to hook up her television, Jack had positively cowered. Greg deliberately thrust the dog away, which seemed to discourage him for the moment. "Anyway, I wanted to see if you would go out with me sometime soon."

"But you live in Richmond."

"Yes, but it's worth the commute."

She fidgeted. How did she get herself into this? Oh yeah, it was Monica's fault. "To tell you the truth, Greg, I have to say that, well, that I'm seeing someone else."

There was a long dead silence and a blankness of expression. Had he heard her?

Then, finally, "You are? Monica didn't mention—"

She cleared her throat, trying to buy time to extrapolate on the lie. "I don't tell her everything. I guess I shouldn't have gone the other night, but I was led to believe it would all be very casual."

"Uh, yes." He still seemed a little befuddled, or was that just the way he was? "But this other guy, who is he?"

"Oh, nobody you would know. He travels a lot on boats. He's in shipping, on ships." She fiddled with her donut, hoping that this extraordinarily weak fabrication was enough to discourage him.

"I see," murmured Greg, still looking confused and remarkably disappointed, "and it's serious?"

"Well, yes, probably, I think."

"You don't sound convinced."

She sipped her coffee, eager to fill her mouth so that nothing else stupid would come out. "No, no, I just don't feel comfortable talking about my feelings. That's all. I'm sorry if you were misled, Greg. You seem like a very nice person."

"No, that's all right. I just hope this fellow knows how special you are." She nodded. "I better get going. I'm expected back at the office." He'd already stood up. That's a business type, ready to cut his losses.

She stood up, brushing a few donut crumbs off her jeans in the process. "Okay, well, thanks for breakfast."

She felt bad. He looked a bit like she'd kicked him. He seemed genuinely disappointed. That was novel, somebody disappointed about losing her. She'd forgotten that there were men out there, unlike her ex-husband. Just for a fleeting instant, she wondered if she was being too rash. After all, there wasn't really anyone else in her life, not anyone real anyway. But again, looking at his so very youngish-looking face, she figured it better to leave things as they were. Never would have worked. Better not to look back.

"I hope you feel better, Hallie."

"Oh right, well, thanks, Greg."

As she saw the boy off, the slightest touch of sadness in her eyes bothered Jack. He wondered if he was being very selfish. Perhaps she did need someone in her life, someone real that she could touch, not Jacob the seafarer or Jack the ghost.

CHAPTER FIVE

La Casa Grande

"*Hallie.*" She opened her eyes. Had someone spoken? She was tired, incredibly tired. She must have dozed for a moment while going over some of the pages she'd written earlier that day. The voice — it must have been a dream. She let her eyelids droop again into that twilight state of sleep.

"*Hallie,*" she began to open her eyes. "*No here, remember I'm here.*" She tensed for a second and then began to relax. The feeling flooding over her was familiar but still cold, so cold.

Jack stood on the small screen porch on the far side of the white, wooden farmhouse.

He was puzzled. There was something out here. There must be. Only moments before, he'd felt the awareness drawing him in this direction. He had left Hallie curled up in the recliner in the den as he and Jack Jr. went off to investigate.

He continued to search around in confusion. There was no one here, but he was sure. It had been so strong.

Turning slowly, he looked suspiciously back into the house. A quick dread spread over him. How stupid of him! It wanted him out. It had made sure he was not around to interfere.

He moved like lightning back through the kitchen into the den but stopped abruptly on the threshold. Everything looked undisturbed as he had left it. Hallie remained as she'd been, still quietly asleep in the chair. Somewhat reassured, he moved to be next to her but slammed smack and painfully into something tangible.

Whatever it was blocked his way. Nothing was visible to the eye, but he would have sworn he'd collided with a massive sheet of ice. He could still see Hallie across the room but was barred from getting anywhere near her. Her head was moving restlessly in sleep. It was evident that she was troubled. He felt panicked and frustrated as hell. There had to be a way to reach her.

Again, he tried with all his might but crashed hard against the psychic wall. He could see her lips moving. She was dreaming another dream. And then something occurred to him.

He moved to the fireplace on his side of the room, sitting on the edge of its black stone ledge. "Not so easy, friend," he whispered as much to himself as to anyone else listening.

He closed his eyes and willed himself to where Hallie was.

Nobody, but nobody was taking her.

It took a few minutes for his eyes to focus. The air was hazy. He waited a moment, but it didn't clear. Everything remained hazy. He breathed in deeply. Oh lord, he looked down between his fingers. It was a cigarette. Bless Hallie's dreams.

He put the cigarette between his lips and inhaled deeply. It felt as though the smoke scorched his throat. But oh, it was good — part of a life almost forgotten.

"You know, you really shouldn't do that. Those things will kill you, eventually."

For the first time, he noticed the woman only a few feet away, leaning against the bar and watching him with hard brown eyes. Her lips were painted dark red, and her eyelashes dipped a little too heavily in mascara. And as he casually scanned downward, it became obvious that her black dress was fitted a tad too tight. But it didn't detract from the tasty vision that was Monica Quimby. Her bleached hair was a startling contrast against the sequined black dress.

She reached up to place the long, thin, white cigarette she held near her brightly polished fingernails between the lips. The lips he was sure she pouted deliberately to entice him. Expertly, she inhaled, seconds later expelling delicate trails of smoke and leaning in closer with a wicked grin. "It'll kill you, but like you should care." She smiled seductively. "We've been waiting for you, Jack. Is it okay if I call you Jack?"

He reached out for a short glass on the bar filled with an amber-colored liquid. "This isn't poison, is it?" He took a swig, just as he suspected — scotch, his drink of choice, or rather it had been.

Monica put one hand on her hip deliberately inching closer to him, so that she could provocatively whisper huskily, or so he assumed. "Now, why would I want to kill my date for the evening?"

His eyebrow rose, or so he assumed it did because he couldn't see it just now. "Your date?"

"That's right, lover, and I'll show you a good time later if you play your cards right."

He breathed in. She smelled of heavy perfume. In fact, she must have taken a bath in it. "So, this was all Hallie's idea?"

She pursed her lips in an annoying way. "Now, that would be telling."

"Look, Monica—" he took another swift drink of scotch and decided he might as well play along until he figured out a game plan. "Forget it. How about we get onto the main event. Where is Hallie?"

"Oh, you are impatient. Are you impatient in everything, Jack?" He didn't like the way she lingered on his name. He didn't know who was in charge here, but his taste in women, even in his former life, didn't quite go this extreme. He half expected her to quote a price for services to be rendered any time now. "Well, all right, if you're sure you don't want to just spend some time with me."

He smiled, "Quite sure, Mon."

She took another puff of her absurdly long cigarette and then extinguished it in the ashtray on the bar. "You better get rid of yours too. Hallie doesn't like people who smoke." She grinned, "OOPS, one strike against you," she giggled annoyingly.

He extinguished his cigarette with deliberateness and a tinge of well-disguised regret. "No problem."

"Ooh, aren't you forceful? Do you like it rough, Jack?"

"I don't know what you're trying for here, Monica. But I've got to tell you, you're getting downright irritating."

"Sorry, I just thought I'd make things easy for you, Jack."

"Hallie?"

"Right, oh, do you like your suit? I picked it out myself. I like my men dressed well."

For the first time, he looked down and noted the dark blue suit he was wearing. It was expensive, as was the cologne he smelled on his skin. Well, at least when he found Hallie, he would have a shot at winning her over. "You look smashing, Jack. You're a handsome man. Why waste that on Hallie?" And then her red fingernails fingered the collar of his starched, white linen shirt. "You're so far out of her league. You need a woman who knows what she's doing. Who's been around."

"The question is around where."

"Now, Jack, that's not a nice thing to say, is it?" she pouted her lips again. "Be sweet to me, or I won't take you to where Hallie is."

He cleared his throat, the powerful stench of her perfume nearly gagging him. "Um, Monica, how about we get out of this bar, and you take me to her. All right?"

"Don't you mean them?"

"Them?"

"Hallie and her date. You don't think she's alone, do you?"

"Ah, no, I suppose I don't." Actually, he hadn't considered that possibility, although it did make sense. Whatever he was dealing with wouldn't have made it that easy for him to get to her. "Well, let's go and see them both. All right?"

"Sure, Jack, whatever you want. But I hope you're not disappointed."

Monica grabbed her little black sequined purse and threw a "Put it on his tab" to the burly Mexican bartender, who made a sound akin to an affirmative grunt. She slipped her arm through his and whispered again huskily, "Come on, Jack. They're waiting for us in the restaurant."

"Oh, is there a restaurant here?"

She snuggled, slinking a little too close to him. But then restraint didn't seem to be a concern with her this evening. Deep down, he had to admit she was appealing in a very sort of basic, primitive way. But he wouldn't be enticed by obvious temptations. He was here for Hallie. That thought actually startled him a bit. He hadn't really acknowledged the gradual, growing attachment he felt for her. But it was true all the same. He was pledged, in a way, whatever that meant in this scenario.

"Haven't you figured out where we are yet, Jack?"

He looked around, really for the first time, scrutinizing the decor. It was flamboyant, colorful. "It's through the door, Jack." Across the room, there was a huge opening. It seemed it must be the connection to the restaurant that Monica had alluded to. He tried to move forward, but she had glued herself up against his side.

"Look, Monica, we aren't going to make much progress this way."

She allowed a slight separation. "Sorry, Jack, I just love being next to that suit you're wearing."

"Wonderful."

She allowed him to walk forward, and they passed through the portal into a loud, crowded establishment. His eyes quickly scanned the walls, which were hung with large, colorful sombreros.

"It can't be."

"I just love this place. You do like Mexican food. Don't you Jack?" And then she added with excess, "It's so hot and spicy."

"This is the place you took Hallie with that Greg fellow and what's his name."

"Richard, but they're not here tonight. Just you, me, Hallie, and her date, of course."

And then, a short, fat, harried-looking Mexican waiter popped out of a cluster of people. "Hola Amigos! Ready to get a table?"

"No, we're meeting someone. In fact, I see them over there." Monica grabbed his arm and literally dragged him through a maze of crowded tables. He was so disoriented by her pushing and pulling amongst small groups of semi-intoxicated people that he didn't see a thing until they were there. She stopped abruptly behind a man with jet-black hair in a dark gray suit. "Well, we made it." The man's broad frame obstructed Jack from seeing beyond him. He rose slowly and turned to face them.

Jack recognized the face immediately from Hallie's previous dream. Samory held out his hand to him. "Glad you could make it, Jack."

Of course, it was all unfolding now. Deliberately, Jack did not shake the hand extended. He was no hypocrite, at least not today. "I never shake the hand of a rival."

Samory smiled and bared a glimpse of his abnormally white teeth. He nodded, "Understood, but I believe you've already been claimed tonight by the adoring Ms. Quimby."

Monica took the cue and squeezed his arm a little too tightly with half of her body. He aggressively detangled himself from the embrace, "Yes, a little too adoringly. Now, where is Hallie?"

Samory smiled again, his dark eyes looking secure and triumphant already. "Why, of course." And then he stepped away so that Jack could finally see the other occupant at the table.

He opened his mouth to speak but was struck dumb by the spectacle before him. It was Hallie all right, but she was dressed only in the old, well-worn, orange bathrobe in which he'd seen her wander around the house, with her hair completely done up in big, round, spongy curlers. Her face was completely devoid of makeup, actually looking a little splotchy as though she'd just woken up. "Why don't you say hello to Monica's date, Hallie?"

Looking completely befuddled, Hallie got to her feet quickly, knocking over the half-drunken strawberry margarita in front of her. Out of nowhere, a tall, skinny waiter appeared and yelled loudly across the restaurant, "Another accident at table five, third one tonight."

Jack saw Hallie visibly turn red. "Sorry, it's just not my night. Nice to meet you, Jack." And then, noting his impeccable appearance, which he sorely regretted now, she added, "Monica didn't really tell me to dress up."

Samory put his arm around her protectively and chimed in, no doubt for everyone's benefit, "That's all right, Hallie. I worship you just as you are."

Jack felt an anger rush in. They were banking on him being shallow, and, damn it, he wasn't that shallow anymore.

He reached out and abruptly grasped Hallie's hand, which, for some reason, he found a little sticky, and put it to his lips, speaking only to her. "I have always found natural beauty much more compelling than that which is manufactured." Then suddenly, Hallie's face squinched up, and she let out a loud — "ACHOOO."

He felt the spray hit targets all over his designer suit and regretfully realized what the stickiness had been.

Samory chuckled beside him, "Looks like you're going to need a napkin, old boy."

Hallie added, her voice now having a definite nasal quality, "Sorry, I have a little bit of a cold."

Monica whispered in his ear, "Sure you don't want to leave now, lover, before little Miss Drippy over there ruins anything else?"

Jack smiled forcefully and patted his suit with the napkin he'd taken from the table. "Not at all," he said, sitting down, "I wouldn't miss this for the world." He noticed Samory's swarthy face perceptively frown, and that delighted him immensely.

They all had half-eaten plates of Mexican food in front of them, all except Hallie. It seemed that the cold had not dulled her appetite in the least. In fact, she was the only one of the four putting away the tasteless fare. He tried hard not to watch her eat. It was obvious to him now that someone was working overtime tonight to present her in the most unattractive light. "Oh, this just is such wonderful food," and then another spoonful and that awful noise she made because her nose was all stuffed up so much like the snort of a—

"Gosh, Hallie, you're eating like a pig tonight," Monica giggled.

She nodded, "I don't know why I'm so hungry." And then she stopped suddenly, becoming aware that everyone's eyes were on her. Her spoon froze in midair, and she looked around sheepishly, slowly letting the utensil descend back to her plate.

"You know what, Jack," Monica cooed next to him. "I would love a dance."

"Dance? I don't remember there being a dance floor here."

She smiled, "Right over there."

He followed her gaze and saw that the wall on the other side of the room when he entered was now gone, revealing a small bandstand filled with gentlemen playing soft Spanish music. "Come on Jack," she nuzzled him with abandon in front of everyone. "Monica wants to dance."

He frowned, and then Samory chimed in, "Yes, Hallie, I would love to hold you close on the dance floor and move to sweet mariachi music."

Hallie turned red, "Uh, I'm too stuffed, Samory."

"Me too, Samory," Jack jumped in. "Why don't you take Monica. She's more than ready."

Monica opened her mouth to decline, but then Hallie added, "Go ahead, Samory. Monica's a wonderful dancer."

Monica grimaced, looking trapped, and Samory grumbled in his foreign accent, "All right, one dance, but I can't bear being away from you too long, Hallie." Hallie smiled tentatively and then sneezed in her food, aggressively wiping her already red nose with her napkin. Samory added without conviction, "I'll be back soon, my darling." Hallie nodded, still miserably rubbing her nose.

With a desperate flourish, Monica threw out the parting line, "Now don't you try to steal my boyfriend, Hallie." Hallie just looked up at her with apparent confusion and a little irritation. As the pair made their way to the dance floor, Jack wasted no time moving into Samory's chair beside Hallie. He grabbed the unused napkin in front of him and handed it to her.

"Oh, thanks, I should have brought some tissues, but for some reason, I didn't plan this evening very well." She rubbed her nose hard. "Gosh, my nose itches."

He smiled, trying desperately to be charming. "That means someone wants to kiss you."

She shook her head, missing his intended hint completely. "Oh well, I guess it's Samory, but I don't know why. I wouldn't want to kiss me right now." He grinned. It was still Hallie. Under all the subterfuge, beneath the curlers, the old bathrobe, the cold, it was still Hallie, "ACHOOOO," as unappealing as she might be at this moment.

"It really is nice to meet you, Jack. I mean Monica has told me how crazy in love she is with you. You know, I don't know why she told me not to steal you," she rambled on almost to herself. It was obvious to him that this whole convoluted situation completely befuddled her. "I mean, first of all, I know how close the two of you are. I mean, she didn't tell me. Well, she told me some, but I mean, I'd never do that to a friend. You know, you don't do that kind of thing to a friend. I mean, not that I could. Good grief, look at her and look at me. She's so together, and I'm—" she paused reflectively. "Well, I'm not."

He frowned. Monica had certainly covered the bases here. No telling what she'd put in her head. This would take a little strategizing, and he didn't have much time. "Well, um, Hallie, you seem like a very honest kind of person."

She looked at him with those soft, brown, guileless eyes. "Uh yeah, I suppose."

"Well, that's why I really feel like it's only fair to tell you that Monica—well, she hasn't been completely truthful with you."

The eyes got wider. "She hasn't?"

"No," he lowered his voice in a grave and confidential tone, "she was too ashamed to tell you the truth, but it has been torturing her. And, well, I can see how much you care about her."

She looked a little panicked. She was buying into it. "I do care. I guess."

"I don't know if I should say anymore."

"Please. What is it?"

"Really, I would be betraying a confidence."

"You must tell me."

"I don't know."

Her eyes were like saucers, "PLEASE!"

He took a deep breath and put on his most pained expression. "It's not me that Monica is crazy about. It's Samory. She's fallen in love with him."

"What?" it came out in a whimper.

"She's afraid to tell you. They both are. They don't want to hurt you."

"Both?" Even softer.

"I'm sorry, Hallie. I felt you should know."

"Oh no," and then "What should I do?" almost directed to the cosmos.

Perfect, "Well, if you want to know what I think."

The eyes came back to him imploringly. He almost felt a bit guilty, almost. "Yes, what do you think, Jack?"

How he liked the sound of his name on her lips. "There is a way you could spare them and yourself," and then he paused dramatically, wondering if this was going to thud like a lead balloon. "You could let me kiss you."

She straightened up, looking suspicious, "What?"

"Yes, when they come over, let me kiss you. That would make both of them think that you've moved on."

With much skepticism, "Don't you think that's kind of quick?"

"No time like the present."

"I don't know." There was hesitancy, maybe confusion.

All he had to do was push like crazy.

He glanced over at the dance floor. The music had paused. "It's so important, Hallie. But you have to make up your mind quick," he added urgently.

"I have a cold."

He looked at her intensely. "Hallie, I don't care."

"It might be catching."

He glanced back over his shoulder. Samory was heading toward the table, his face animated by a broad smile. He turned back to Hallie. "I'll risk it. Come on, be bold, Hallie."

She looked at him with a touch of skepticism, and then a new expression, one of curiosity, passed over her features. It sort of made his heart stop for a moment, and then miraculously, she nodded. He reached over to her and softly touched the sides of her face with his hands.

Her skin was warm — maybe a fever from the cold. Gently but passionately, he began to kiss her. Merely an instant after the first contact, his plan was forgotten. He forgot about Samory and Monica and the whole ridiculous situation. All that existed was the sweet sensation of her lips, her breath — the rich breath of life. The kiss deepened, and his arms went around her, pulling her closer. The feeling was the sweetest, most intense one he could ever remember. He was home with her, really home, and damn everything else.

And then he was back home, Hallie's home, in front of the fireplace in her house. She was awake, sitting straight up in the chair, rubbing her eyes. She looked completely disoriented. "I have the weirdest dreams," she murmured.

Evidently, whatever had instigated the dream had ended it rather clumsily.

He looked around triumphantly. Standing up, he walked toward her. The icy wall had vanished. It had retreated for the moment.

For him, the experience had, at minimum, been extremely informative. He knew now that Samory was not really his adversary. He had seen him twice, but whatever was lurking around this house had deliberately avoided making an appearance.

And secondly, whoever it was had misjudged him — throwing Monica at him as though he would abandon Hallie for whatever the dream Monica was offering. Clearly, "it" was not all that bright, and that was comforting to him. He wasn't outmatched. This was winnable.

Hallie was walking around the room now, lost in thought, looking extremely bothered. She was thinking about him now. He could feel it on his skin, or what felt like his skin. He smiled. *"It"* had done him a favor. He was becoming real to her now, not Jacob McFarin, not Sir Jacoby, but plain old Jack, who had kissed her tonight. He desperately wanted to reach out and kiss her again, but he knew she wouldn't feel it this time. And that crushing reality markedly tempered his triumph.

CHAPTER SIX

Dear Jack

*S*he stood on the terrace of her father's villa, gazing upon the starless sky of the Paris night. It was as though the light had gone from the world everywhere. She felt desperate and trapped but was not sure why.

It had to be this man, this new presence in her life. It couldn't possibly be Samory, not her love. She heard the heavy step of his boots behind her and knew that, once again, he was taking the opportunity to invade her private thoughts. "What is it, Gabriella? Why do you seem so sad?"

She spun around boldly to face the man who had, against her will, insinuated himself into her life. There were still the remnants of tears running down the alabaster white of her cheeks, but her soft eyes leaped out with fiery sparks of anger. "You certainly *worked hard to win over my father tonight, Captain McFarin, with the grand tales of your seafaring voyages. He is an old man, and it is unkind of you to use him as a pawn in this game you are playing."*

His blue eyes sparkled in evident admiration of her spirit. "I am glad you have a strong will, Gabriella. You will need it to break free of the monster that has you in his grip."

"Samory is not a monster. Stop calling him that."

He came closer to her, taking her small white hands once again in his powerful ones. "His deeds have been monstrous, Gabriella."

She looked down, unable to face the intensity of his gaze. "He has done what he must to survive."

He grasped her chin, forcing her to look at him. "Then, if he is powerless to stop himself, we must stop him ourselves."

Her eyes widened with fear, "What do you mean, sir?"

There was cold determination in his handsome face now. "He must be destroyed, Gabriella."

"No!"

"For his own good, but more so for yours. I am determined that he will not have you. Even at a cost to myself, he will never have you."

And then he pulled her into his arms and kissed her with a savage tenderness that forced all other thoughts to blur away in the midst of their mutual passion.

Hallie grimaced. Maybe not. Maybe this kiss came too soon. And what would her Sebastian Winter books be with no Samory? But she had to protect Jacob McFarin somehow. Why exactly that was, she wasn't sure, only that she liked him too much. She didn't want to let him go. Samory wouldn't have him.

But how could she have them both?

She sighed deeply. This was so depressing. She really had to get a life.

Her head throbbed. She closed out the file and began shutting down the computer for the night. She'd figure this out later. She wondered who her Great Aunt Marie would have chosen. And then she smiled. Aunt Marie would have taken McFarin in a heartbeat. She liked her heroes strong, determined, and not shadowed. But Hallie was different. Always, it seemed, she had been drawn to the complexities, the shadowed mysteries, the comfort of illusion. At least, that was how she used to feel.

Now, it almost seemed as though something was changing, shifting inside her, and she had no earthly idea why.

Jack sat beside her, watching her silently, plotting, wondering how it all would end—knowing that he, too, had pledged to save Hallie, even at great cost to himself.

It was nearly nine o'clock. Jack was playing around at her feet as she sluggishly sipped her second cup of coffee. Every now and then, she absently nudged him away as his sharp little teeth began to sink through her slippers, and she began to dimly notice their contact with her flesh. He was in that teething mode like babies go through, or so she was told. She had resigned herself long ago to the fact that there wouldn't be any children in her life. There had almost been a baby with Edward, but she'd miscarried early on, which probably had been for the best. Otherwise, Edward would have told her what to do and how to raise their child for the rest of her life. And, well, for the child, needless to say, it would have been a poor environment for a child.

Yes, this slow morning seemed flooded with dalliances of what-might-have-beens and her incessant reweaving of the worn-out threads of regret. What would it have been like to have a child with another man? One who wasn't so intensely dissatisfied with her — one like, and then she stopped herself. She looked down at the small puppy playing beneath her kitchen table.

It was the dream. It bothered her. That was part of the reason she was so tired this morning. The dream, or remembering it, had kept waking her up during the night. It was one of those stupid ones like when you're in a swimming pool and suddenly realize you forgot to put on your swimsuit. And, of course, there is no way to sneak off without everyone seeing you. It was one of those silly dreams, completely not grounded in reality, except for one part. There was a man there. The rest of the dream had blurred into obscurity in the light of day. All except for him, this presence she had felt.

She closed her eyes, and the vision of his smiling face rose up before her. He was a nice-looking man, not remarkably handsome like the stuff of fiction, but with short brown hair, a nice, wry sort of smile, and warm blue eyes that somehow beckoned her in the memory.

It was ridiculous, but she couldn't get him out of her mind — the touch of his lips, the comforting but thrilling sensation when he kissed her. She rubbed her eyes. Damn, why couldn't he be real? She smiled glumly down at the dog. And his name was Jack. She remembered that his name was Jack.

She scratched her little furry Jack behind the ears, and he growled in appreciation. The dream Jack and she could have made nice children together — nice, laughing, unpretentious children. But he was just a dream, and all this was, well, extraordinarily depressing.

The phone started ringing, and she went without interest over to the kitchen counter to pick it up.

"Hello."

"You sound like hell."

"Oh, thanks, Monica. Good morning to you, too."

"Did you have a late night last night?"

"No, not really, I just didn't sleep very well."

"Were you alone?"

"What?"

"I spoke to Greg."

"Oh, I see," putting the pieces together. She groaned inwardly. Good lord, she wasn't in the mood to deal with this.

"So, you're seeing someone. Greg says some guy who's in shipping or something. Don't you think you should have told me this?"

"No, not really," she yawned unintentionally.

"Look, I go to all this trouble to set you up with Greg and—" Her pitch was getting strident and nearly painful.

And then a thought popped into the building chaos.

"Monica, do you know someone named Jack?"

Silence, "You mean other than your dog?"

"Yes, a man, a person, maybe someone you work with."

"Well, um, there's a Joseph something down in accounting."

"No, no, it has to be Jack."

Another silence and then dripping with suspicion, "What's this about Hallie?"

"I'm just trying to find someone."

"What about the shipping guy?"

"Oh yeah, well." What about the shipping guy? Whoever the hell he might be. "That's an on-again-off-again thing." Didn't she sound shallow and highly in demand?

Steely and calmly, "Well, then Greg."

"Nope, not Greg. Absolutely not."

"He likes you."

She was getting nowhere — it was time to close this down. "Look, I need to go. We can talk later, all right?"

"What's going on with you, Hallie? You're really beginning to worry me." Actually, she sounded more perturbed than worried.

"I'm fine. I've just got to figure out some things."

Hallie was stretched out on her bed, working on a letter. Jack was lying beside her contentedly breathing in the smell of her hair. She washed it with some vanilla-scented shampoo, and he loved it. Why? Probably just because she used it. He loved being close to her, watching her expression. Maybe it wasn't particularly productive, but he was peaceful doing it.

She was scribbling on a yellow notepad. She should be working on the book. Not long after Monica, her editor called wondering when he could expect her first few chapters. In a few days, she'd told him. It was feasible, but she was so unsettled about the course of the book, about so many things. So, she decided indulgently to pour out her anxiety-ridden heart to her newfound, invisible friend.

Dear Jack,

(It began)

He leaned over and indulgently kissed her softly on the cheek.

I know this is sudden, but I really need a friend right now. And since you're not here to tell me I'm wrong about everything, you're the perfect candidate.

He smiled, a silent confidant. That didn't sound so bad.

I've always been accused of being impractical. That was my ex-husband Edward's daily litany. "You are foolish and impractical, Hallie." I've often wondered why he married me at all. He seemed so absolutely dissatisfied with me all the time. Monica said it was because he felt he could mold me into what he wanted. Isn't that funny? I mean, why didn't he just marry a lump of clay?

He frowned. He couldn't for the life of him understand how any man could see Hallie for anything but the sparkling bright, dazzling person that he saw now. He would give just about anything to spend five real minutes talking with her, laughing with her, just being with her. He slumped back on the bed. He was depressing himself.

Anyway, it was tough, real tough, for me to accept that all my years with Edward were a wash. And shamefully, I will admit I tried to become what he thought I should be. It was the easiest way to keep peace but so exhausting. I was just so tired all the time. It plain wore me out. And I became something I really hated. I was boring. Edward's molded Hallie was boring, not someone I'd want to sit down and even have a cup of coffee with.

He couldn't imagine having a cup of coffee with Edward, except perhaps to throw it in his face.

And Jack, I made the mistake that I thought I never would. I thought for a while that if there were just children, then maybe it could work out. I'm ashamed of it, but I felt like such a failure. He told me what a failure and disappointment I was to him, and I bought it. Thank God there weren't children, but now there won't ever be and—

She stopped. Why was she opening all this up? This was so pointless, dredging up all the old pain, making it raw all over again.

Tears were running down her face. And it pained him terribly to see her so upset. How could he help? He'd never bothered to help anyone before. And now, how could he help anyone the way he was?

He was angry and overwhelmingly frustrated at the state of things. Then it clicked in, the one thing he did always have going for him — his unyielding determination.

Gently, but with purpose, he reached out and softly touched her cheek — touching her tears with his fingertips. He could actually feel their moistness on his skin. It was physical. And then, for just a flicker of an instant, everything became different. It seemed for a moment that everything around them stopped. Hallie froze and then pulled back unexpectedly. Her face reflected genuine surprise, almost as though she had felt it, too.

Her hand flew up to her face on the spot where he'd made contact. "What's happening?" she whispered out loud. "What's happening to me?"

"What's happening to me?" Gabriella peered with trepidation into the oval mirror atop the dark mahogany-wooden dresser that her father had ordered specially constructed for her by an artisan in Lyons.

The soft brown eyes staring back at her were troubled deeply. The presence of Jacob McFarin in her house tonight had shaken her more profoundly than even she had thought possible. Out of a semblance of decorum, she had slapped his face, but it was with a mixed and confused heart. And she felt in the core of her soul that he knew it as well.

She wrapped the light cotton robe covering her nightgown more tightly around her. The evening was warm, even balmy, but her flesh was chilled, chilled by her wavering spirit. There could be no denying it now. She was beginning to doubt Samory.

Hallie hesitated. It was strange. Her fingers were actually trembling. She had no idea where this was going. Impatiently, she turned around, half-expecting to see someone behind her, bending over her shoulder, and she was surprised in some part that there was not. What on earth had gotten into her? She returned to the screen, consciously brushing away the doubts that were creeping inside her mind, the ones questioning her grip on reality.

Jack stood quietly beside her. She had looked right at him, directly at him, with expectation in her eyes and then disappointment. If only he could find some way, some stronger way, to breach the barrier between them. The fact that the barrier was life itself at this moment seemed only a minor complication.

Perhaps he was not the man that—that he had represented himself as. Perhaps Jacob was being honest. Perhaps all that she had come to believe, to trust, was really a fabrication, a thin veil covering the truth.

A chill swept through the room, and the pale pink candle on Gabriella's night table almost flickered into oblivion. She turned slowly. In some measure, dreading what she knew she would see. The balcony door was ajar, and Samory stood in stillness on its threshold. For the first time at the sight of him, Gabriella's heart traitorously clutched with fear. He reached out to her with his hand. "Why have you come to me like this, Samory?"

"It is time, Gabriella, that you become mine for all eternity."

She stood up slowly, fighting the almost unendurable compulsion to surrender to his will. "But Samory," she hesitated, each fiber of her being battling with every other fiber of her being. It was horrible, torturous, unbearable, until all she could truly manage to utter was, "Uh."

There was silence. His bright red lips curled into a frown. "What was that my dearest?"

The words once again choked back deeply within her throat. "Uh," she forced out another try, "Ahh, ug."

He stood there quietly, almost frozen, eyeing her with a measure of irritation.

Hallie paused, "Shit." Gabriella couldn't stand there continuing to gurgle nonsense. She had to say something, but what?

And then suddenly, as though providence had reached in to save her, there was an intense pounding on her door. Bam, bam, bam, "Gabriella are you in there?"

She opened her mouth to reply, but all that continued to come out was, "Uh, uhh."

And then, in the flicker of a heartbeat, the door violently crashed open, splinters of wood flying in disarray everywhere. And there, Jacob McFarin stood on the other threshold with his rapier drawn. "I sensed that you were in great danger, Gabriella. So, after dinner, I waited in the bushes until I saw a creepy mist collect around your balcony."

Samory was expressionless, except for one eyebrow that rose in disdain, "Gabriella, who is this buffoon?"

Thank heavens she had found her voice, "Samory, ummm, this is Jacob McFarin. He's a seafarer."

"McFarin," he grimaced, "Now, where have I heard that name before?"

The reckless adventurer pointed his sword directly at Samory's heart. Although not convinced that he possessed one, uttering with suppressed rage, "Perhaps you remember my sister, Margaret McFarin."

This was the first flicker of significant emotion that evening that Gabriella had detected in Samory. She could see in his eyes that, indeed, he recognized the name. "Margaret, Margaret was very dear to me."

"Was that before or after you killed her, you scoundrel?"

Samory's deep voice seemed to resound throughout the room. "I wanted her with me, always, but she was not strong enough."

Gabriella was stunned and perturbed, "Samory, you truly loved her?"

"Not as I love you, my darling. There has never been another as you."

"What a crock of shit that is," Jacob spat out. He continued rapidly, "How many have you said that to?" and he added with emphasis, "This week?"

Samory's ebony eyes blazed with fury. "I have had enough of you. You insect!"

He reached his hand outward, which, before their eyes, mutated into a hideous claw. Gabriella jumped back and screamed maniacally, "No!"

Hallie repeated, "No."

Jack whispered next to her, "Yes, a claw, an awful, horrible claw."

She shook her head, seemingly battling with herself, "No, no. He wouldn't have a claw. He's not some kind of bird."

"Of course, he's a bird. He's a bat. That's a bird."

"No, a bat is a mammal, not a bird."

"It has a claw."

Emphatically, she reiterated, "No claw, something else, how about hmmm."

He frowned, women and their pickiness. "All right, then how about a paw?"

She stopped and considered, "A paw? I'm not sure that would—"

"Dracula ran around like a wolf, and wolves have paws."

She clicked her fingers nervously on the keyboard. It was amazing to him how rapidly his words were reaching her. Of course, she assumed they were her thoughts, not planted ones. But the rapport was undeniably getting stronger.

"A paw doesn't sound so scary."

He nodded, "Yes, that's right. A claw, a big nasty claw is much scarier."

"I suppose I could take it out in a rewrite."

"Absolutely."

"Okay, let's give it a try."

Gabriella screamed, and Jacob jumped back just in time to avoid the swipe of Samory's monstrously mutated hand. "What are you doing, Samory?" Gabriella pleaded, with terror fracturing her voice.

"I'm not letting you go!" The voice that came from him was not the smooth, deep tones of the man that she thought she knew, but the sound of a horrid creature bellowing forth from no other source than the bowels of hell. He reached toward her with another hand that had also become the extremity of a beast, a gargoyle, a—

"That's enough Hallie, we get the picture."

She nodded in agreement to her invisible source of inspiration and then continued.

Jacob leaped forward, pushing Gabriella out of harm's reach as he deliberately hacked off one of Samory's monstrous claws with his sword.

It hit the floor of her bedroom, bursting into combustive flames as it dissolved.

The monster that was once Samory bellowed, "Do you think that you can take her from me so easily? I was here long before you, and I will outlast you, you depthless coward? Relinquish her, or I will destroy you both!" And then, he dissolved into the air, slipping away quietly as a light mist dissipating through the balcony door into the shadows of the night.

Jack looked at Hallie. She stared glassily at the screen, breathing deeply. Something else had fed her Samory's final declaration. He'd felt it. The presence had made that threat and made it to him directly. It wasn't giving up, wasn't surrendering, and there was no way now that he could either.

CHAPTER SEVEN

Crossing Boundaries

Monica circled the den of Hallie's house with deliberation. Her eyes peered at every inch of the room as though there was a hidden truth somewhere that she could penetrate. Jack wondered why she had popped in on her friend, although he used the word loosely. She had professed it to be a social call. But her actions, her stance, her determined expression, spoke of something else. She was, without question, a woman on a mission.

"The coffee will be ready in a few minutes." Hallie entered smiling but eyeing Monica with the fringes of suspicion. Evidently, she was getting the same vibe. Jack settled on the couch so that he could have a ringside view of whatever was about to unfold.

Sitting gingerly in the rocking chair, Hallie motioned to the recliner beside her. "Why don't you have a seat, Monica." She added, "You look like you're about to jump out of your skin." Jack smiled. He did appreciate Hallie's directness. It could sometimes be less than tactful, but he did find it terribly endearing.

The blond settled herself on the very edge of the chair, poised it seemed to spring into action if the moment was called for. Hallie frowned, "I was surprised to see you in the middle of a workday. You didn't lose your job, did you?"

"No, I didn't lose my job," she snapped back with thinly suppressed irritation.

"Okay," she cleared her throat. "Is it Richard? Are things not going well there?"

"No, well, we broke it off, but that's not really what's bothering me."

She waited for elaboration, but there was none. "Then, what is it?"

"It's Jack."

"Excuse me."

"Yes, I know it sounds strange."

"You're not talking about the dog?"

"No, not your dog, Hallie."

"You know another Jack?"

"No, not really," she shifted uncomfortably on her perch. "What about this seaman person you're seeing, Hallie?"

Hallie's eyes had become wide with interest as she zeroed in on the target. "No, no, never mind that; tell me what you were saying about this, Jack." Then she tacked on, "I mean, you have me curious."

Monica leaned in closer to her, her well-lipsticked mouth poised in hesitation, "I have to say. It just doesn't make much sense."

"That's okay," Hallie delivered very calmly. "What is it?"

She took a deep breath, obviously finding whatever she had to say particularly troublesome. "Well, ever since you mentioned that name, I mean, other than the dog, I've been thinking. And it's been bugging me, kind of irritating me, actually. And then suddenly, pretty much out of nowhere, I remembered why."

"Why?" Hallie was leaning toward her, literally on the edge of her seat, sort of feeling that she wanted to spring up and rip the words out of Monica's throat if need be.

"This is the strange part. I remembered a dream I had."

Hallie leaned back in her chair as a measure of understanding began to flood across her face. "Tell me about it," she said softly.

"Usually, I don't pay any attention to dreams."

"What happened?" The voice was quiet but filled with determination.

"In the dream, we were back at this restaurant, you know, the Mexican one."

"Ah huh," softly.

"And I was all dressed up, and you. Well, you didn't look so good."

"Go on," with little emotion.

"So, anyway, we both had dates. And yours was this exotic, dark, foreign-looking man — very handsome, striking, and, well, just compelling. And mine was this other guy."

"What kind of guy?"

"Well, he was nice-looking, sort of, not extraordinary like your date." Jack bristled a bit at her evaluation. In his day, he had been highly thought of by the opposite sex.

"He was dressed really nice and for some reason in the dream well—"

"What," she reiterated, "what happened!"

Monica looked at her with a bit of confusion. "Why is this so important to you?"

Hallie smiled forcibly, trying to reestablish the appearance of composure. "I just want to know what happened. You have me on pins and needles."

Monica continued, seeming momentarily satisfied that she had her friend's rapt attention. "Well, in the dream, I was totally nuts about this guy — my date, I mean. And he's really not my type at all."

"I see."

"But that's not the strange part."

"It's not?"

"No, the strange part is that his name was Jack, and then you ask me if I've ever met someone named Jack. Isn't that bizarre? I mean, what do you make of that?"

Hallie was still for a moment. Then, she smiled and shrugged, "Sounds like an interesting dream."

"The name, doesn't that mean anything?"

"Well, it's a common name. I wouldn't stress too much about it, Monica."

And then her small eyes squinted smaller, "What about your Jack, Hallie. The one you were looking for?"

"I didn't find him." Now intent on shifting gears. "Do you want that coffee now?"

Monica stared back at her, looking a little befuddled. "Are you sure this doesn't mean anything?"

Hallie smiled, but her thoughts were elsewhere. Jack could tell. He could feel it. She was moving closer to him. "It's just one of those strange coincidences, nothing to worry about, nothing at all." She murmured this to placate Monica, but her words were filled with no conviction whatsoever.

He remained on the couch in Hallie's den after the ladies had left, wondering what in blazes to do next. "Did you call?"

He glanced up. Great Aunt Marie was across the room looking out the window. "She drives a jaguar. Never liked them myself, but I suppose it suits her." She looked at him and smiled, "Been keeping yourself busy, my boy?"

"Things are getting complicated," he uttered with a deep sigh.

She nodded, "Well, that's an understatement. You've got Hallie here, almost believing that you exist and the other. Well, let's just say you've got it enraged."

"How do you know?"

"Hard not to. Can't you feel the anger seeping out from the walls around here? *It's* hopping mad all right. So, if I were you, I'd watch your back. No telling what *It's* liable to do next."

He grimaced, "That makes two of us. I have no idea what my next move is. That's the problem. Maybe I'm making things worse for her here."

"Do you think so, Jack? It's nice to think about what's good for someone else for a change, isn't it?" She smiled indulgently, "Didn't do that much before, did you?"

"Try never."

She nodded her cherubic face in a comforting way. "Must have been a lonely life."

"It didn't seem like it at the time. But now, well, it's hard to imagine living that way again."

"Too bad you didn't recognize all of this then. Maybe things would have been different."

The sadness of what might have been seeped into him for possibly the first time. "Yes," he murmured almost to himself. "Maybe things would have been different."

"Well, chin up. There's still a lot of good you can do here."

"But I can't figure out what the best thing to do is."

"Then stop using your head. In my experience, it's not too reliable. Feel what to do. That way, you won't go wrong."

"Aunt Marie."

"Yes."

"Do you think I could have made her happy? If things had been different?"

"Without question, my boy," she said without hesitation. There was a different expression in her clear, blue eyes — one that he found difficult to read. And then she repeated, "without question."

It was three o'clock in the afternoon, but Hallie had pulled down all the shades in her bedroom until the interior had the appearance of dusk. She had silenced the ringer on her cell phone and had put on her most comfortable pajamas. Of course, she realized it was somewhat ridiculous to consider sleep at this time of day. But she also realized that there was no course for her now except this one. Whether or not this was a rational course was not the issue.

Jack curled up in his doggy bed near the door where she'd placed it. She was grateful he was taking the hint that it was nap time. It seemed better to keep him near so that he wouldn't be agitated by her absence.

She stretched out on the bed and closed her eyes. "All right, Jack, if dreamland is the only way I'm going to find you, then here I come."

He lay down next to her on the bed, hopeful and determined that he could deliver what she was after.

CHAPTER EIGHT

In Dreams

Hallie awoke from reality. Looking around and slowly allowing it to sink in, absorbing the impact of where she found herself, left her feeling distractedly gratified and somewhat cautiously pleased with her accomplishment. There was no question that this was a dream, but it was unlike any other dream she could remember having. This dream was the product of a conscious creation, an active choice to be here. She smiled, relaxing a tad. It was here, all hers, even down to the specific place.

Not because she particularly liked it here. In fact, she was developing an acute distaste for the environment. But this place was a touchstone. It was where she'd seen him, the man she sought.

The waiter who had just approached her smiled broadly. "Will you be dining alone, ma'am?"

She shook her head, "No," and then tentatively added, "at least I hope not."

He ushered her with exaggerated flourish to a corner table. Her eyes scanned the restaurant. It was indeed Monica's favorite Mexican joint, La Casa Grande, but there were subtle differences. The atmosphere felt quiet, more sedate tonight, unlike the raucous place she remembered. These were Hallie's touches, her influence. For the first time, she glanced down and became aware of what she was wearing. It was her red dress, the pretty one — the one she had saved for that special some time. Evidently, this might be just that special night, bizarre as the circumstances were.

"Can I get you a margarita, Ma'am?"

She considered carefully, "No." She must maintain a specific mood, "I think tonight I'd rather just have a glass of white wine, chardonnay."

"Yes, Ma'am," and then he was gone, and she was left with her thoughts for company. She looked around pensively, the first flush of success beginning to dim a bit.

A few couples were in the restaurant, but they were seated far from her, nearly not even touching the fringes of her reality. None of them remotely resembled the man from her dream, Jack. She turned the name over in her mind, Jack — and then again, hmm, Jack? Here she was, having another dream, hoping he'd show up.

The soft, lilting music of a mariachi band played in the background. The stage was certainly set. Everything seemed to be going without a hitch. All was well. She was in control of the moment. She took a breath, holding it for what seemed like an eternity, and then let it escape in a deep rattling sigh. A wisp of panic trailed across her heart. It was more than possible she would spend the evening here in control all by herself. What if this whole thing was a delusion on her part, and she was just certifiable?

Hadn't Edward once accused her of having a thin grip on reality? Didn't this just support all his accusations of her? Of course, the truth was that it was Edward's reality she could never manage to get a grip on.

She shook her head with resolution, control, control. She wouldn't, couldn't think about Edward tonight. Where was that glass of wine?

What are you up to tonight, Hallie?

Nothing much, I'm trying to find this guy that I met in a dream once. But that's not crazy, is it? No, indeed, it's absolutely ludicrous.

She slumped forward, covering her face in her hands, feeling all her masterful control draining away. It seemed hopeless. She was hopeless — ridiculous and hopeless.

And then she felt the warm pressure of a hand on her bare shoulder. Tentatively, she looked upward and found herself gazing into warm blue eyes. "I got your message. I hope I'm not late." Her heart clutched painfully. Good Lord, it was him. Here he was, smiling at her as though they were old friends.

How weird was that?

It hit her in a flurry. It worked. Her experiment worked. She couldn't believe it. What did she do now? She opened her mouth to speak but, like her counterpart Gabriella, was struck completely dumb at the moment. Truly, she hadn't planned this far, just as far as getting him here. He was here, but what would she do with him now? Deep down, she didn't really think that this would work, that he was real on any level. Things that she wanted just didn't come to her.

She glanced up. Yes, he was still there. He was dressed casually but nicely — a white shirt with khaki pants. He seemed to be waiting, perhaps waiting for her to speak, but she hadn't. Frankly, it was all too much. He shrugged a bit, seeming to be amused by her reaction. "That's all right." He sat in the chair next to her and deliberately pulled it closer to hers, again acting as though they were well acquainted. "I imagine this must all seem very strange."

Then there was the interruption, the sudden appearance of the waiter bringing her wine, further splicing into the confounding moment. "Here you are, Ma'am. And what can I get for you, sir?"

"That looks good. I'll have the same." He nodded and disappeared quickly. Hallie still mute, just observed the transaction silently and with wide eyes. He seemed very relaxed here, this Jack person, quite comfortable in this bizarre circumstance.

He was looking at her now, intently. Seeming — how could she say — quite pleased, as though he'd just won a lottery or something.

Why was that? After all, they didn't really know each other except for that kiss. Did he remember that? How exactly did this work?

He reached over with familiarity and took her hand in his. Maybe he did remember. It was a small gesture, but the contact sent tendrils of pleasant sensations up her arm. Good grief, what was this? He, too, was taking his time to speak, apparently trying to choose the right words. "You know, Hallie. You haven't said anything since I arrived."

"Yes, I know that," she managed to get that much out. Genteelly extricating her hand, she took a sip of wine. Even if it was a dream wine, she needed something to help her get hold. She glanced back at him. He still seemed amused. What was so damn funny?

"I've been looking forward to spending time like this with you for a long time, Hallie." He spoke softly and gently as though he was taking great care with her.

She took a difficult breath. "Is that so?" And then she tacked on as an impulse, "So you spend time like this often?"

She emphasized the word this. It was a simple question but jam-packed with a million other questions just beneath. He nodded, frowning just a tad, she thought. "Yes, I suppose it must seem a little, well, out of the ordinary to you."

"This," she gestured outward, "nooo, I meet some of my favorite people dreaming about bad Mexican restaurants."

He smiled, "Can I count myself in that category? I mean the favorite people part, not the bad Mexican restaurant part. That's not really my fault." She looked down. She couldn't help smiling. Wasn't this all pretty silly? "I have to admit, Hallie, that I was a little disappointed you picked this place."

"Oh, well, sorry about that. I wasn't quite sure where to make reservations in a case like this." His eyes were sparkling.

He was admiring her. She could feel it somewhere inside her skin. And their conversation, it was slipping into an easy banter like in one of those romantic comedies she had in her DVD collection. It was something she recognized but had never experienced before. Of course, it was still her dream.

He took her hand again and, this time, brought it to his lips, kissing it softly. She stared at him, a little stunned at his boldness. What was he doing? She liked it, but what the hell did he think he was doing?

She tugged on her hand again, but he seemed intent on not giving it up this time. "Now, let's just slow down here for a minute, Jack. It is Jack?"

Those eyes, gorgeous blue eyes were just piercing in intensity, "Yes, it's Jack, Hallie." And then, ignoring her protestations, he kissed her hand again, and little shots of pleasure seemed to shoot out across her skin.

She had to clear her mind. She clumsily and abruptly yanked the hand away this time. "Now look, I'm a little confused here," she cleared her throat awkwardly. "No, that's not true," she said without looking at him. Those mesmerizing eyes could make her forget what she had to say. "It goes way beyond just a little. Who and what are you? I mean, really, what is all this?"

Undaunted, he quite smoothly wrapped his arm around her shoulders and pulled her a little closer to him. Again, the tingles of electricity trailed up and down her at the contact, particularly where his hands touched her bare shoulders. Dream or no dream, she knew men, well, a little bit, and there was no question that he had an agenda where she was concerned. He whispered to her, "That's a whole bunch of questions, Hallie, and I really don't feel like answering them all right now. Can we just say I've been trying to reach you for a long time, and I want to make the most of our time together?"

She found it difficult to breathe just now. Her loudly thudding heart seemed to be interfering with the respiratory process. "Um, well, Jack. I know this is a dream and all. And I do admit I instigated this, sort of. But I really think that's not going to do it. I'm going to need a bit more of an explanation. All of this is so very," she swallowed, "unusual."

He lightly kissed her cheek, "Did I mention how beautiful you look in that dress, Hallie?"

"Um, no, you didn't. Thanks." Now, what was she trying to say? "But well, my life is kind of going crazy, and I'm not sure why, and I thought if I could find you, well, maybe we could talk about it." She looked up at him plaintively. "What do you think? Do you want to talk?" The waiter appeared out of nowhere, postponing his reply.

"Well, here you are, sir, your wine. And—" He paused, critically surveying the situation. "Ah, I can always spot newlyweds."

Hallie straightened up, startled by the intrusion. "Uh, no, it's not what you think."

"I see," he said with an expression that indicated he did not approve. "Well, I'll be back amigos to take your order in a few." She had a sinking feeling that her masterful control of this situation had definitely slipped a few notches.

"Take your time," Jack interjected. "In fact, take a long time."

Hallie couldn't suppress a giggle. She giggled when she was nervous, and right now, she was way off her nervousness scale.

Jack, well, seemed certainly determined. And she liked that, she thought. She definitely liked a determined man. Just wasn't sure if she could handle a determined man. "Well, what do you say, Hallie? Do you want to get married tonight?"

His eyes were sparkling again in that mischievous way. "Excuse me. Perhaps we could get past the first date." Did she say the first date? Did this bizarre circumstance really constitute a date?

"I'm serious."

"You're crazy. I don't know you, and you're probably not even real," she rambled unconvincingly.

He smiled. Did he have a bit of a dimple? Gosh, she really liked that. "That's the beauty of it. We can do anything we want to tonight."

"No, no, I need at least six months to plan, plus picking out flowers and caterers. Maybe the Mexican band over there might be available for the reception. But on second thought, they're probably booked solid," she noted with purely frivolous sarcasm.

"You want me to check?" She was laughing with him. Now, how did that happen? "Well, then, if not tonight, how about spending the next six months with me in this dream?"

"Don't they have a word for that, like coma?"

"Is there anything that you really want to get back to?" She felt a measure of heaviness creep into her. It felt a little like reality. Maybe he was right. It wasn't much of a life. She frowned, "I have a dog and—" she paused.

"Two sick plants." He nodded, looking a tad less enthusiastic, "I know."

Her eyes widened suspiciously, "You know? And how is that Jack, that you know? And what else do you know? And why?"

"More questions." He shrugged, "I know you like peppermint tea, spicy buffalo wings, and writing late at night."

Her head was whirling. This was just too weird. Of course, all of this was just too weird. "I guess you must know this because I made you up, but then how did Monica know about you?"

The smile left, "I know this is strange, Hallie, but you have to believe that you didn't make me up."

"Of course I did. There is no other explanation."

His voice lowered and sounded just a tad irritated to her. "There are other explanations."

She grimaced, digging in a little with her own obstinacy. "Oh really, well, I haven't heard anything that makes sense yet."

He patted her hand and solemnly said, "Hallie, you have to believe me."

"Oh," she paused, "and why exactly is that?" challenging calmly.

He sat back, looking a little frustrated, but then his face seemed to set with a kind of inward resolve. He reached over and pulled her closer to him. "Does this feel real, Hallie?"

And then, in the next second, he was kissing her — softly at first, tentatively, and then not. It became passionate, more intense, until everything around her blurred away, everything except him. By the time the kiss ended, she didn't know what was real or much less care.

"Who are you?" she whispered, then adding with a degree of desperation, "And where the hell have you been all my life?'

He answered with another kiss — this one almost desperate and savagely passionate. She didn't care one bit that they were in the middle of a restaurant. She didn't care that he would probably disappear when this dream ended. All she cared about was that his arms were around her, and everything and everyone else could go to hell.

"Sir, sir! Do you realize that you are kissing my wife?"

She literally froze in Jack's arms. And then shakily looked up to see the figure that matched the voice towering over them.

"Oh God," she whimpered. "It's Edward."

Hallie could tangibly feel the frustration in Jack's body as he delicately ended their embrace and stood up beside her ex-husband. He glared at him with what could only be described as seething anger. "So, this is Edward?" Hallie nodded, straightening out her mussed-up red dress. "Great! I've been wanting to meet this lousy son of a bitch."

Jack knew he was moving quickly, but his instincts told him deep down that his time alone with Hallie would be minuscule. So, instead of romancing her, he'd decided to put some fast moves on her. And actually, all was going exceptionally well, that was until the ex-husband showed up.

"Who is this man, Hallie?"

She was absolutely confused and befuddled. After all, wasn't this her dream? What the hell was Edward doing in her dream? "I—"

"You don't have to answer him, Hallie." Jack jumped in with evident irritation. "Eddy is your ex now."

The tall, lanky, blond man, whose features were bland enough to blend in with his pale complexion, looked angry. At least, he looked as angry as Jack had ever imagined he could get. Sizing him up with little objectivity, there was no doubt in his mind that this was one cold fish. He couldn't fathom what Hallie had seen in him. Of course, in all fairness, he couldn't fathom some of his own choices. "Sir, I don't know what delusion you are operating under or worse, perhaps what fabrication my wife has conveyed to you, but we are still married."

Hallie stood up. Her head was beginning to hurt. "Edward, what are you talking about? We're divorced."

He put his long, thin hands on her shoulders and squeezed them in a nearly painful manner. "No, Hallie. Don't you remember? We decided to give the marriage another chance?"

Jack was highly perturbed. In fact, beyond perturbed, he was downright incensed. He wanted someone to pay for this interference. Of course, he realized that this manifestation was, in all probability, not Edward, but that didn't stop him from wanting to punch his block off. He grabbed Edward's hands and forcibly, trying to deliberately inflict a little pain, removed them from Hallie's shoulders. "I have a bulletin for you, pal. It's not going to work out."

Hallie smiled. She couldn't help it. This was chaos, crazy chaos, but she admired the way Jack was sticking up for her. It did feel good to have someone in her corner for a change. From where she stood, she could see that the tips of Edward's ears were red, in fact, beet red. That delighted her. It had always been the signal that Edward was really angry.

"Hallie, I insist you stop this now and come home to discuss this."

"Discuss it with yourself, Edward." She spat out with new-found and exhilarating courage. Why, she was convinced that she could rumble with the best of them. "I'm not going anywhere."

"This is just like you, so irresponsible—"

Jack whirled Edward around and grabbed him by the collar of his highly starched shirt. "Do you really want to continue this? Because I really and mean really would like to mess up your face. Although, in your case, it might cause some improvement."

"Yes, officer, that's the man. I'm sure of it." The Mexican waiter had suddenly returned flanked by two highly overweight police officers.

Without ceremony, one unsheathed a gun and pointed it directly at Jack. "Sir, please, unhand the hostage."

Jack sighed deeply. *It* was truly pulling out all the stops tonight. "The what?"

Edward squiggled nervously in his hands.

The officer repeated, "You heard me, sir, unhand the hostage."

"He's not a hostage. He's an idiot."

Edward chimed in pitifully, "It's true. He'll kill me. I know it."

Hallie couldn't believe the mess that was ensuing in front of her. "Shut up, Edward. Don't be ridiculous. Officer, this is a big misunderstanding."

"No, Ma'am, you don't understand. Mr. Sanchez called us once he recognized this man from his copy of the ten most wanted list."

Jack frowned, still maintaining his grip on the squirming Edward. "And that's something you keep with you?"

"Oh yes, sir, right up in the kitchen. So, I don't hire any bad people."

Jack nodded, "Ah."

The police officer continued, "Yes, Ma'am, there's a reward out for this one. He's a killer, a swindler, and a flesh peddler."

"A what?" Hallie exploded incredulously. Jack rolled his eyes.

"Yes, Ma'am, I have a witness here with us to identify him as the mastermind of one of the biggest brothels in Mississippi."

Jack turned, highly irritated and mildly curious. "You have a witness here! Now? From Mississippi?"

"Yes, that's right. She's been sitting around for months waiting for you to be apprehended. May I introduce Ms. Monica Leray?"

"Monica, who?" Hallie exploded again with even more incredulity.

As if on cue, Monica approached sauntering up from the back of the restaurant in an impossibly tight-fitting black leather mini dress.

The officer continued, "Ms. Leray was one of Mr. Brennan's most successful call girls."

Monica stopped in front of Jack, smiling seductively and blowing him a kiss. "Sorry, Jack, but I had to make a deal to save my own skin."

Hallie stood there stupefied at the impossible scenario in front of her, and she could not believe that just a few moments earlier, things had been going so well. "Jack," she began softly. "Is this true?"

His eyes widened, and then he fired back at her. "No, it's not true. It's ludicrous!"

Hallie paused for a moment's reflection. For her, these seconds between were the eye of the storm. Here, indeed, was a pivotal moment. There was a choice at hand, either to try to wake up and end this fiasco or take control of her own destiny.

In an instant, it was decided. With deliberation, she took a careful step backward until she was beside the second pudgy police officer who had yet to contribute a word to this mess. His pistol was hanging openly in its holster, somewhere in the vicinity of his sagging middle.

For a brief second, she met Jack's eyes, enough to draw courage from them, although she felt sure he didn't have a clue what she was contemplating. Springing into action, she grabbed the gun and pointed it at the armed policeman. "Freeze, fat boy," she yelled. "Drop it, or I'll blow you into your next life."

The policeman looked at her with confusion, "Ma'am?"

"I said drop it." And to Hallie's intense pleasure, he did.

Jack looked at her with a mixture of admiration, disbelief, and, of course, intense desire. What a woman! She sent him a dazzling smile, "Come on, Jack. I'm rescuing you."

He released the trembling Edward and took her hand.

"You've already done that." The two ran out of the restaurant into a night of possibility.

Monica watched them leave, smiling with a touch of envy. "Must be real love," she commented to no one in particular.

CHAPTER NINE

Jack Brennan

She didn't know where he led her, and for the most part, she didn't care. She just felt alive and free for the first time in, well, probably for the first time. Hallie had dropped the gun somewhere along the way. It didn't seem to matter much as they flew through the cool night in a convertible. She'd never been in one before but secretly had wanted to. The car they escaped in seemed to be the last of her influence. After that, the power had shifted, or rather, the control of the dream. She knew that. Things had gone crazy inside the restaurant, and then she had relinquished it all to Jack. Somewhere outside of Monica's Mexican dive, he grabbed both her hands and said, "Trust me."

And she did, without words. She had placed herself in his hands wholeheartedly without reservation — just content to enjoy the heck out of the wild ride they were on.

For a moment, as they drove through the night, Hallie had closed her eyes and felt an incredible pull. Something was trying to draw her back to her house in Virginia, but she resisted it. She wasn't ready to return. Going back would mean leaving the man beside her. And for some reason, she didn't want to verbalize; she was enormously reluctant to do that just now.

When she opened her eyes again, they were driving through a busy, traffic-filled city she didn't recognize. It was still dark, still the middle of the night, she assumed.

"Where are we?" she said.

He put his arm around her, pulling her nearer to his warm body. "We're in my town."

They parked on the side of an impressively tall, shiny building and headed toward its extravagantly large brass-accented entrance. Jack had his arm around her as he ushered her forward. "It's all right," he whispered in her ear.

As they entered, a man in a bellman's uniform greeted them almost at once. "Good evening, Mr. Brennan. We've missed you here, sir."

"Thank you, Wallace. I've missed being here." Hallie looked at Jack's face. Something, a sadness, lit across his features.

"Are you all right?" she asked as they headed to a nearby elevator.

He kissed her softly on the cheek, never letting her stray very far from him. "Yes, I just haven't been home in a while."

He didn't know quite what to expect when he opened the door of his 14th-floor New York City apartment. He'd done well as a cooperate lawyer, made plenty of money, lived in a nice place, and drove a nice car, but he had lived a life that now seemed in most respects to have been absolutely futile and aimless.

He kept holding Hallie close to him. Because he was all too aware that, at any moment, the dream could end. He was a bit incredulous that it had not already. *It,* whatever the hell *It* was, had pulled out everything and the kitchen sink to ruin him in Hallie's eyes. But she had seen through it all — a *flesh peddler,* who even used that term anymore, of all things? Well, *It* was definitely not a master at the art of subtlety.

Somehow, he had gained control of things in the dream. It was an oddly empowering feeling, and it had been his choice to bring her here — a place from his old existence. It was familiar ground, and perhaps, he hoped, she might just breathe some life into something that seemed so barren for him now.

He unlocked the door with the key he had found in his pocket. It swung open, and dusty impressions of the past flooded toward him.

She looked in quiet and wide-eyed. "This is your place?"

"It was," he murmured.

He flicked on the light switch that cascaded across the den's ceiling in a series of strobe lighting. The decorating was stark — modern, with brass, white, and black furniture and a large tropical fish tank built into the wall. She walked in by herself, leaving him behind, slowly turning around, quietly soaking in all the details. He didn't disturb her — just watched as she stopped in front of a turbulent painting of the ocean on a far wall. Ironically, it had been one of his favorites. "You like the water," she spoke aloud but almost to herself.

"Yes," he moved beside her. "I've always wanted to live near the water."

She smiled a little sadly, "Me too." And then she turned toward him and laughed with more bewilderment than genuine humor. "Why does this seem more real than my own life right now?"

He rubbed his eyes and noticed for the first time his face was rough. He was unshaven. How long had it been since he'd thought about something as simple as that? And how long would it be before he would again? "I don't have too many answers for you, Hallie."

She looked at him intently. What a joy he felt in knowing she was seeing him, the real him, no matter the context.

"But you do have some answers, don't you, Jack?"

He couldn't deal with this yet. He walked to the sliding glass door across the apartment. "You haven't seen my balcony view of New York City."

"That sounds like an evasion."

"I'm a lawyer. Evasions are my specialty."

She smiled softly, "Now there's a dribble of information."

"Come on. I wouldn't be the proper host if I didn't show you something breathtaking tonight."

She laughed, "That you've done a few times."

He opened the sliding glass doors and led her into the cool night. It was all as he'd left it. Even the plants needed watering. She rested her hands on the pale brick of the balcony's ledge, again deep in some impression that this place was creating for her.

There was a breeze that fluttered her dark hair softly around her shoulders. She had never seemed so beautiful to him as she did at this moment. He tried hard to engrave the image in his mind. He knew that such gifts for him would be sparse. "It's beautiful, Jack. You were right, absolutely breathtaking but lonely somehow. I was wondering what a boy who loves being near the water is doing stuck way up here in the middle of a city."

He answered dismally. "Playing the game, I suppose. Thinking that this made me some kind of a success."

She eyed him thoughtfully. "I see. My knight in shining armor is some kind of a wheeler-dealer."

"Maybe that's who I used to be."

Her eyes, dark in the shadows, were focused so intensely on him filled with her innocent wisdom. "Who are you now, Jack?"

He touched her face with his hand just for a moment, just to be near her warmth again. "There are things I want to say to you, Hallie, because I know I'll never get to otherwise."

"I don't understand this. You keep acting as though you know me so well, but we don't really know each other. Do we?"

He pulled her closer, touching softly the sides of her face with both his hands. "What else, Hallie?"

"This can't be," she seemed so troubled. He could feel it through just touching her skin. "It's impossible, but I feel like you've been near me."

He was torn. His mind, his sharp, analytical mind, was telling him that he had to stop. That telling her too much wasn't right or fair. But his heart was dragging him into a different arena, a terribly hazardous one. Could she live with knowing that the new man in her life wasn't even alive anymore? Was ostensibly just a ghost? She grabbed his hands with hers. "You've got to help me, Jack. All of this is driving me crazy, and the book I'm trying to write. Good grief, it's insane, but I feel you all over it and—" she stopped, her voice choked up with tears.

He stroked her hair gently, desperately trying to soothe her somehow. All of this was flying way out of his control. "It's all right, Hallie."

"And my God, your eyes Jack, I've seen them in my mind in a character I put in the book." He pulled her face to his and kissed her passionately, trying to silence the growing panic in her voice.

She pulled away, tears running down her cheeks. "Why can't you just tell me what's going on?" she pleaded.

"I can't, Hallie. It would be too hard."

"Why? Why would it be too hard? I don't understand. Is it something awful?"

She had no idea how she was torturing him. "You don't understand, Hallie. I want to protect you. I want more than anything for you to be safe and happy. I've never cared about anyone else as much as I care about you. I've never put someone else before myself before." She was breathing hard, still crying. He kissed her tears. "Please, Hallie, I don't want to make you sad."

She was shaking her head. "It's not fair. Nobody has ever cared about me that much. Nobody has ever made me feel like this, so much. Why can't it be simple? Why can't we just be together? You're not someone I just made up. I know that. I would feel that if it were true. Jack, please, there must be some way."

He held her tightly and kissed her face over and over. "I want that more than anything, more than anything," he whispered.

And then again, with an amazing strength, she pushed him away. She looked almost angry with him. "Then what is it? Tell me who you really are. I'm not a person who can just trust blindly anymore. Why do you keep talking about the man you used to be, Jack? What do you mean?"

He was surprised and a little shocked by the fiery woman standing before him. There were so many facets to her, and how he ached to uncover each and every one.

He turned away and looked for a moment at the grand skyline of the city before him. This he really hadn't missed much. He'd never truly felt like a part of it, and that hadn't changed.

"Damn it, I'm strong enough to hear it, Jack."

He saw her face illuminated in the artificial light cascading off the building. It was true. She was strong, stronger than anyone he'd ever known. "I know that, Hallie. I just don't know if I'm strong enough to tell it."

There was an infinite silence between them, and then she said quietly, "Try."

He couldn't suppress a smile. She stood there waiting, solid, prepared for the worst. And God help him he was about to deliver it. "Hallie, the thing is—"

He had no idea how to get into this, how to soften this. There was another endless gulf of silence. "What is the thing, Jack?"

"You see, not so very long ago, I lived here."

"I got that."

"Well, good," another pause, "and then something happened to me."

"What happened?"

She wasn't missing a beat. It was nerve-wracking. "I was out there in the rat race, like always, trying to hustle to get to a meeting, and then—well, I got sick." The memory felt so vague and insubstantial now.

Her voice was soft and measured. "What do you mean, sick?"

"I mean," his own voice sounded very flat to him. "I had a heart attack."

Her face melted over with concern. She reached out to touch his arm with sympathy. "Are you all right now?"

He cleared his throat, "Not exactly."

More concern, "What? Were there some kind of complications, Jack?"

He considered this, "Yes, I guess you could say that. There were definitely complications."

She waited patiently, but in the moment, he wasn't elaborating. "Like what?"

"Well, Hallie."

Her face was very serious but intensely caring. He could see it in her eyes. Already, somehow, she'd woven him into her life. She had claimed him as her own. He belonged to her now.

"I can handle it, Jack." He knew it was true, but that did not lessen the despair of delivering his news.

"I didn't recover, Hallie, from the heart attack. That was my last day as the old Jack Brennan."

She smiled with hesitation, "The old? What do you mean? Who are you now?"

He knew nothing would be the same, but there was nowhere to go but forward. "I'm dead, Hallie. I'm a spirit, a ghost, whatever you want to call it, but I did die that day."

Her face seemed frozen with that partial smile, and then she spoke, "I don't understand."

"It's true," he stated flatly.

"You mean, you're really dead," she said with a nervous little giggle.

"As much as I hate to admit it."

She just stared at him blankly for a minute, then looked away. "Well, Monica certainly would get a kick out of this," she whispered. The comment seemed directed to no one in particular.

It wasn't quite the reaction he'd expected, but under the circumstances, who the hell knew what to expect. "And as a ghost, you've been—"

"Well, actually, I've been living with you in your house."

"My house?"

"Yes, in Virginia, you, of course, can't see me, but I've been there ever since you moved in. The little dog, he sees me." He tagged that on. Why? He really couldn't say.

"Oh Jack, well, lucky him. And I have to go to sleep to see you." She nodded absently as if at a loss for words, then, after an awkward second, turned and walked back into the apartment.

He followed her, more than concerned about the calm way she was taking all of this. She sat down on his couch and stared forward as though lost deeply in thought.

"Hallie, I've been trying to reach you for some time. I've had some success with your writing."

Softly, "My writing?"

"Yes, I've been giving you ideas."

"Jacob McFarin."

"Yes, he was my idea."

"Well, that explains his eyes, I suppose." Her voice was vague. Maybe it was the shock of it all.

"I suppose," he echoed.

"So, you want to get rid of Samory? That's your idea, Jack?"

He sat beside her. Man, he didn't want to get into this yet. "Well, that's complicated."

"And this isn't?" She smiled sadly, "This one may be tough to work out, Jack. Are you sure, though, are you positive you're dead?"

He reached out and took her hand, wanting desperately to hold onto a little of her warmth. "I'm afraid so. It was selfish of me to tell you. You could have gone on thinking I was just a dream."

"You are a dream," she whispered. "You're the man I've always looked for."

"Well, I guess I've always been awkward with timing."

She smiled bleakly, "Awkward? Your timing sucks. Couldn't we have met before the heart attack?"

Ah, the truth, "You probably wouldn't have liked me much then."

She squeezed his hand. "And where you are now. Is it nice where you are, Jack?"

He shook his head. He could actually feel her thoughts gravitating in a dangerous direction, "Don't even think about it, Hallie. There are rules, and that would be breaking a big one."

"But you don't understand, Jack. I don't want to be without you. I don't want to go back to a life without you. I feel as though, somehow, I've been looking for you for a long time. And now—" She couldn't finish.

He put his arm around her and pulled her snugly next to him. "We'll fix this somehow, Hallie."

She laughed, "Maybe I could just go into a coma and spend all my time with you."

"Maybe we'll find a miracle," he whispered to her.

"Are there such things still around?"

"I found you, and that's been a miracle."

"Smooth talker." She shook her head and leaned with despair against his shoulder. "What are we going to do, Jack?" And then she smiled grimly, "Maybe we could hang out here for a few thousand years."

He nodded, seriously contemplating the idea on one level. He murmured, "I know some great take-out restaurants."

"Or I could cook. I like to cook but just not Mexican. I think we've worn that out."

"Yes, at least that much is certain."

And then, there was a forceful knock at the door, making Hallie perceptively jump in his arms. "Oh God, it's the police."

Jack said suspiciously, "No, they would probably say open up. It's the police." How irritating! He was in no mood for any more surprises tonight.

"But who could it be?" she whispered to him.

"In this dream, I wouldn't cross out anyone."

Cautiously, they both walked over to the door, and Jack bent to the peephole quickly and then straightened up. "Who is it?" Hallie whispered more loudly.

"It's your Aunt Marie."

"But she's—" And he answered with a shrug.

A voice from the other side of the door shouted crankily, "Is anyone going to let me in?" Jack swung open the door, and Aunt Marie smiled, beaming at Hallie, looking just as she remembered her from her youth. "How's my little green apple?"

Still looking shocked, Hallie bent forward and allowed the plump little woman to hug her.

"Aunt Marie, I'm so happy to see you, but what are you doing here?"

"Oh, didn't Jack tell you? He and I have become good friends?"

She shakily looked at Jack, "No, he didn't."

"There's a lot I haven't gotten to tell Hallie about yet."

"Well, why don't you invite me in for a brandy, and we'll all sit down and have a chat. You do have brandy, don't you, Jack?"

"Yes," and then he added, "At least, last time I checked."

Hallie sat on Jack's white-and-black checked sofa and watched as her Great Aunt Marie, sitting in a black leather lounge chair, sipped a glass of Napoleon Brandy. She did remember her aunt having imbibed from time to time, but she also remembered being a teary-eyed teenager attending her funeral.

And then there was Jack — Jack sitting right next to her, holding her hand, squeezing it occasionally, sending pleasant shivers up her arm. Jack, whose blue eyes melted her to her very core, yet did not possess a respectable gene in the decorating department. Even in her distracted state, his black-and-white motif truly made her want to puke. But that was okay. That was fixable. But the being dead thing, this was another matter.

For just a moment, Aunt Marie stopped sipping. "Yes, Jack, I certainly have to say you've got good stuff."

Hallie cleared her throat, determined in a fashion to make sense of the senseless. "Aunt Marie, as happy as I am to see you, I can't help but wonder why you're here. And well, how do you know Jack?"

"Oh yes, Jack, well Hallie, I met him at your house."

"My house? Oh, you mean because you're both." And then she stopped, not wanting to utter the words.

"Operating on a different spiritual plane."

"I see." That must be the politically correct version. "Yes, but here the both of you are," she added grimly, "in my dream."

Jack squeezed her hand again. "I know this must all seem strange to you, Hallie."

"Strange, I don't know, Jack," a little disgruntled. "Does this seem strange to you?"

"Well," he paused, "yes," evidently not wanting to elaborate.

"Hallie, dear, there is an important reason I've popped in here, other than to visit."

She took another sip of brandy, then continued, "Dear, I know being here seems like a good thing, but it's actually rather perilous."

"What do you mean?" Jack jumped in with concern.

"Well, while you two are off gallivanting, so to speak, what's left of Hallie is still back in her house, unprotected."

"What do you mean what's left of me?"

"Your body, dear. It's still in your bed, vulnerable, while your spirit—"

"My spirit?"

"Yes, that's what's traveling around in this dream state, creating alternate realities. Your spirit and, well, Jack's too."

"So, what are you telling me?" She was putting the pieces together now, "that I need to go back?"

Her extraordinarily round, cherubic face looked very serious and very wise, an expression Hallie remembered well from her younger days. "Yes, I'm afraid so."

Hallie turned to Jack, but he was silent. Whatever he was feeling just now, he didn't seem to want to share. "But Aunt Marie, you don't understand. There hasn't been enough time. I'm happy here with Jack. I feel, in a way, like I'm home with him, like it's where I belong. I don't want to go back to the way things were."

"I'm sorry, Hallie, but more things are at stake than you know. Your spirit has a path that it's chosen as has Jack's. You can't just circumvent that to, well—"

"To be happy?"

"I know it's hard to understand."

"It's impossible to understand." She stood up. Suddenly, she felt as though she couldn't breathe. This was all too much. "Excuse me." She left them and walked back out to the balcony.

She looked into the night sky, unwelcome tears dripping down her face. There weren't nearly as many stars here as in the country. At least she couldn't see them. The lights of the skyscrapers blocked them. She didn't really like the city, but she knew she would gladly stay here with him, anywhere, to be with him. She felt his arms go around her waist and his head rest against her shoulders.

"I'm sorry," he whispered to her, "I should have let you go on believing I didn't exist. I was selfish."

"I'm selfish too. I don't want to go back."

She turned around. Those blue eyes she so speedily had grown to adore weren't sparkling now. They were steely and determined. "Hallie, if there's a way, I'll find it. I promise."

"But I still have to leave?"

He nodded reluctantly, she thought. "For now."

She stared at him, desperately trying to visually devour every nuance of him, memorizing every aspect so that she could bring him back to her mind whenever she wanted.

And then she kissed him with everything in her, trying hopelessly to stretch a moment into eternity.

CHAPTER TEN

The Chill

She felt something wet and sticky on her face. Her eyes fluttered open, and then she felt something furry nuzzling her neck. Just for a second, her heart clutched in fear, and then she remembered it was Jack, or rather Jack the dog. She sat up in the bed. It was daylight outside. The clock on the night table reflected 7:30 a.m. Apparently, she had slept through the night.

Jack continued to try to lick her face, but she gently nudged him away. "It's just you and me again, boy." Her eyes slowly canvassed the room, looking for a trace, anything, but there was none. She pulled the puppy to her and held it against her heart.

It squirmed playfully, but it was the closest thing to Jack that was here right now. She whispered, "If you see him, boy, tell him I said hi." She then wiped away some tears that seemed to want to become a fixture on her face.

Jack was frustrated, frustrated as hell. He had watched Hallie all morning moving through the house, attending to mundane activities like making coffee, feeding the dog, and doing the dishes with a lethargic, absent quality. He could feel the heaviness in her heart, feel it acutely because it mirrored his own.

He was an idiot. How could he reach her, tell her all about himself, and then leave her like this? It was absolutely maddening, and then there was the other matter.

When he returned, it was like walking into an icebox, a spiritual icebox. While they were gone, something had permeated the walls of this place so much that he could barely breathe, or rather, the impression of breathing that he'd been functioning with. Apparently, in spending the time away, they'd surrendered some ground, and *It* had wasted no time taking advantage of it. Even Jack Jr. was having trouble finding him amid all this foggy, chilly muck that *It* had spread throughout the place.

He had to find a way to dispel it. But the gloominess of Hallie's mood, and his to match, would make it doubly hard or so he felt.

"I told you there was trouble."

Aunt Marie was standing beside him. "It's like a freezer in here. Does Hallie feel it?"

"Not really the same. To her, it just feels like a heaviness. And, of course, she thinks it's just because she misses you."

He looked at her with concern. "Did I make a mistake? Letting her know who I really was?"

"It doesn't matter whether it was a mistake or not, Jack. It was a choice. One you have to make the best of somehow."

"How do I do that?"

"Well," she paused reflectively, "I don't know. I've never been in a situation like this before." He waited for more, but there wasn't.

"That's it?"

"No, I've never been in love with someone not on the same plane of existence as myself. It's a unique situation you've got here."

"But don't you have some answers? You have been, well, on the other side for a while."

She nodded, now evidently following his thought train. "That's true, and I do know some things. But I'm still learning about others. Crossing over doesn't make you all-knowing, as you can attest to my boy."

Well, that much was true. He didn't feel like he knew much more than that day in New York City when it had all ended for him. "This coldness, what is it?"

Her usually cheerful face was frowning now. "It's energy, negative energy. Your shy friend was enraged when you ran off with Hallie and that it wasn't strong enough to prevent it. So, it spent some time brewing about the whole matter. And since no one was here to stop it, all that soaked through everywhere.

Those of us in the spiritual state can release a lot of energy, good or bad."

"So, how do I dispel it?"

"Well, you've got to spread positive energy around to counteract it."

"And how do I do that?"

"Good question. Good luck with that, Jack."

He grimaced, super. At times, the old lady's presence just seemed to add to his frustration. She told him just enough to drive him crazy. How could he lighten things up around here?

Hallie sat curled up in her lounge chair, just staring blankly ahead. She was thinking about him. He could feel it. And then he had an idea.

It was mid-afternoon, and Hallie sat at the computer feeling antsy. She truly wasn't in the mood for writing. She started to stand up but felt the pull again — the insistent tug to come here that had been gnawing at her all day. She clicked her fingernails on her wine glass. It was her second glass of wine.

She hadn't really wanted wine. And then she stopped, "Jack?" She spoke out loud. Maybe she really was crazy. "Jack," she began again, "I guess you're trying to help, I guess, but I'm just too cluttered to write." She started to stand up but felt a pressure on her shoulders. It was almost physical, but in all fairness, it could also be construed as her imagination. "Please, Jack, if this is you, I just want to go watch TV or something. I haven't got it in me to do this right now."

She felt her fingers tingling, itching to hit the keyboard. Damn it, if this was him, he was relentless. But right now, being pushed just made her feel more stubborn. After all, he was the one turning her life upside down, what life she had. And then, she felt a soft breeze pass through her hair. The air conditioning wasn't on. It was actually a cool day for summertime. It tickled a little. What was he doing? Looking down at the keyboard begrudgingly, "All right, I'll try, but it will be crap. I know it."

Gabriella's head ached terribly. Somehow, Jacob had gotten her away from Samory, but she could not begin to recall just how it had happened. Somewhere, in the midst of her terror, she had lost consciousness.

And she awoke in unfamiliar surroundings. She was stretched out on a bed in a sparsely decorated room. And Jacob stood near a far window, rinsing his face in a porcelain-washing basin. With embarrassment, she suddenly realized that he had removed his shirt. She sat up tentatively, but her head continued to ache with every movement. "Where am I?" she whispered.

He turned around, drying his face off with a towel. "I'm glad you're awake, Gabriella. I was on the verge of calling a physician." He moved to the only dresser in the room and retrieved a cup that he brought to her. "Here is some tea that Madame Guillard brewed for you."

"Who?"

"The kind lady that has been renting this room to me."

She took the warm cup into her hands and began to sip it. It had the smell of rose petals and peppermint. It did taste soothing. With a sudden concern, she inquired, "But who did you tell her that I was?"

He sat on the edge of the bed, staring at her with his liquid blue eyes. Even in her present state of ill feeling, they disturbed her to a degree that even Samory had failed to elicit within her. "Why, the only thing I could. I told her that you were my wife."

Hallie paused. Her heart was beating ridiculously fast. "Jack, this isn't me, so it must be you. Where are you going with this?" With much uneasiness, she returned her hands to the keyboard.

"You told her what?"

"It would not have been proper for you to be here under any other conditions. So, I told her an untruth. An untruth that I hope will come to pass before too long."

She looked away from him, feeling a blush creep beneath her skin. "Where is my father?"

"I encouraged him to leave the city for a short time. I convinced him that I would protect you."

"From Samory?"

"With my life, Gabriella, I am pledged to it."

The horror of the night before came rushing back to her. "How did we escape him? The last thing I remember."

He took her hand that was trembling uncontrollably. "Fortunately, he retreated. But there is no assurance that he will again. He wants you and is determined to have you, Gabriella. So, we must frustrate him at every turn."

"How do you mean?"

"Once we are married, I believe the thread of control that he retains over you will be snapped."

She straightened up, "Married? I have not agreed to marry you, Captain McFarin."

He grasped her other hand warmly in his. "Gabriella, I have already gained your father's consent as well as made arrangements with the priest of St. Michel's cathedral."

She forcefully pulled her delicate hands away from his much larger, coarser ones. "That is all very well, Monsieur, but there is one person, a very important person, whose consent you have neglected to obtain."

He grimaced, "Yes, well, I have always had the habit of mastering the simpler tasks first and building up to the more complicated ones."

"That is a failing on your part," she retorted with spirit.

He smiled knowingly, "I have heard it described as a charm."

"Evidently, sir, you have been listening to the wrong people."

Even in her weakened state, she was determined not to let him get the best of her.

She made a motion to get up from the bed, but her head began to spin with dizziness. Gently, he pressed his hands against her shoulders to pressure her down again. The warmth of his touch was almost more dizzying than her injuries. "Gabriella, you are not well enough to get up yet. You must allow me to take care of you."

The beat of her heart was quickening again. He was so very near her now, and she could see closely his strong, rippling, muscular chest. Leaning even closer, he whispered to her, "What kind of proposal would be most acceptable to Mademoiselle?"

Her head was still spinning, but it was his nearness now that continued to increase her disorientation. "But you scarcely know me, Captain Mc—"

"Jacob, Gabriella. "He was holding her hand again but strok-ing it intimately in a way that sent tingling shots of pleasure up her arm.

She looked up at him shyly and hesitantly. "But you don't love me, Jacob."

And then he brought the palm of her hand to his lips and gen-tly kissed it. The effect was devastating. No one's touch had ever brought fire to her veins before as his did. "You are wrong. I have known from the first moment that I saw you that you were the woman who had walked in my dreams all of my life. I thought that I had come to this foreign land to exact revenge for my sister's death, but the truth was that I came for you. To save you and to claim you for my own."

"Jacob," she whispered. But it was too late, for he had cut off her words with his lips, his mouth, his sultry, insistent, passionate kisses.

And she knew that she would deny him nothing. Even as an ordinary mortal man, his will over her was more binding and more powerful than Samory's could ever hope to be.

Hallie took a swig of her wine. "Aren't you laying it on a bit thick, Jack? His will over hers, please. All the independent women of the 21st century will balk at that." But she couldn't help grinning. In an overblown kind of way, it was horribly ro-mantic, and it made her weak in the knees, and it made her wish Jack was here in the flesh so she could kiss him again and again and—

"Rrrrrrrnnnng"

The sound jolted her out of her romantic musings. A little shakily, she picked up the cell phone on her desk.

"Hello."

"Hallie."

She waited. The voice was distantly familiar. "Yes, who is this?"

"Well, I suppose I deserve that. It has been a while." And then a coldness clutched in her stomach. It couldn't be, not right now. She said nothing. "Hallie, it's Edward."

Quietly, "Yes, I was coming to that conclusion."

"I hope it's all right that I call you."

She drummed her fingers beside her wineglass nervously. "I just can't imagine why you would be calling me Edward. Everything with the divorce was tied up a long time ago."

"Well, that would be a shame indeed if that were all that was left between us."

She said nothing. She didn't know what to say, couldn't even begin to imagine what he was driving at. Experience had taught her that with Edward, apparent or not, there always seemed to be an agenda. "Are you still there, Hallie?"

"Yep," she rustled a few papers on the desk, "and actually swamped under with work right now."

"Yes, your writing career. I've been following it with interest."

"You were saying why you were calling."

"That's my Hallie, to the point."

She was irritated and feeling curiously trapped. Old habits seemed to die hard with her. "Well, I'm not your Hallie anymore, Edward, and frankly, I'm not up to having an idle conversation with you just now."

"Time has certainly roughened you around the edges."

"And you haven't changed at all," he laughed at her remark in his slightly superior manner.

"Actually, I'm going to be in your vicinity this evening. And I wanted to invite you out to dinner."

"How did you—"

"Your sister was kind enough to give me your number some time ago."

She frowned. Where was this coming from? "Edward, given our history, I don't think—"

"I've always felt that I wanted us to remain friends after the divorce, Hallie, and I never was able to quite bridge that gap with you."

"A lot happened, Edward."

"Yes, but I think as adults, we could manage to spend one pleasant evening in each other's company."

"I really don't—"

"Don't say no to me, Hallie. If it's a fiasco, then at least we can say we gave it a try."

Her head was beginning to hurt. "The thing is, right now, I don't really want to give it a try."

"I know how obstinate you can be, darling. I was married to you long enough. But I think you owe this to all the years we were together. I'll even meet you there. I heard of a good Italian place. You know, in the college town near your little city."

"Edward—"

"How about seven? Marcello's, I think it is. Do you know it?"

"Yes, I do."

"So, I'll see you there. I insist." And then he hung up, not waiting for a reply. That was so like him. It would serve him right if she stood him up. But then he would probably show up out here. Damn him, now she was intensely irritated. It was probably better just to go and cut things short. She didn't want to deal with ghosts from her past when she was, well, dealing with other ghosts. The timing really stunk.

She got up, heading into the bedroom to find something sedate to wear. Jack remained behind. This was some kind of move in the chess game he'd been playing with this thing. *It* was striking at vulnerabilities, at Hallie's. And it really bothered him that she hadn't turned him down flat. Damn the bastard, he obviously still held some kind of control over her. And even contemplating that possibility was making him crazy.

CHAPTER ELEVEN

Edward

She brushed out her dark brown hair as she watched in the mirror. It was a little longer than shoulder length. What had he said? Oh yes, that was right. Edward liked her hair short. It was more sophisticated and respectable for a woman her age. How old was she then? She was only twenty-six at the time. Calmly, she pulled her hair into a large barrette, letting the tendrils escape and fall softly around her face.

Why are you doing this? Why are you going at all? The whispers resounded in her head. And she couldn't help wondering if they came from her or somewhere else.

As surely as if he were standing next to her, she knew that Jack disapproved of this. He did not want her to go. For the most part, she didn't want to either, to step back into a place that had been so painful.

But Jack wasn't here to stop her. He wasn't here to explain to her why it was wrong and why, in some small but significant way, it was a betrayal of him. All of that was made up of small whispers in her mind, wisps of truth that could easily be pushed aside.

Why was she going? She had the power of free will to say no to him.

Partly, perhaps it was curiosity. She was curious as to what had become of him in the four years that they'd been apart and more than that curiosity of what she'd become — what she would be now as she faced him.

Chances were this was foolhardy, and it would all come to nothing. But she would go and face him, the man who had been so instrumental in altering the course of her life forever.

There would be no Jack to protect her, no Jack to stop her from going, and in some strange, silly way, she was angry with him for that. It was something he had no power over, but on a level, she was truly miffed.

Hallie wore a black linen jumpsuit. It wasn't sexy, wasn't conservative. It was simply unique. She wore a set of mother-of-pearl earrings that her mother had bought her and the heart necklace from her Great Aunt Marie. She had nothing from Jack — no pin, no scarf, no ornament of his devotion. It would have been nice to wear something he'd given to her, to show as an outward symbol that she was devoted. She was, for whatever that was worth.

It was a quiet, dimly lit restaurant. When she arrived, she could see Edward sitting at a table across the room. From where she stood, she could even see that he had already ordered a bottle of wine and an appetizer. As she paused in the entranceway, a cold creeping chill of anxiety traversed her spine.

There he was at his table, sipping his wine and eating his food. With a sudden rush of clarity, she wondered what in the hell she was doing.

Jack was heartened by the hesitation on her face. Standing closely beside her, he whispered, "That's it, Hallie. Leave the cold-hearted son of a bitch out there on his own. He doesn't deserve you, not even five minutes of you." But before she could begin to sort it out, the waiter was beside her inquiring about a table, and she was allowing herself to be led to Edward.

As she approached, he stood up to greet her. He was dressed in a dark blue suit, even though it was the summertime. It was one of his favorite colors — suit colors, at any rate.

Hallie didn't recognize this one, although it didn't differ from his old ones all that much. She'd always thought he probably would be content to have a closet full of dark blue suits. "I was beginning to wonder if you'd make it," he commented with little warmth.

"Me too."

He smiled thinly with his thin, pale lips. "Well, I suppose I deserve that." He would make an effort to be charming tonight. She knew, as surely as she stood there, that he had now categorized her as something to be won over.

He'd pulled out a chair for her. There were the manners — slick, good manners, and she'd sat down tentatively. She did notice he'd looked at her outfit but hadn't commented. Compliments from Edward had always been hard to come by.

As he'd settled in across from her, she mentally took inventory of him. He looked essentially the same, perhaps a few extra lines turning downward around his mouth. His skin was still that extra pale, sallow color. His eyes, well, they looked as she remembered except perhaps a little less reflective of light, but then they could have always been like that. She wasn't sure. The memory of those years now seemed so insubstantial and blurred.

Jack had settled down in a chair between the two at the small table. He could feel Hallie's nervousness, and it bothered him. In fact, he could practically feel it seeping into him. It was extraordinarily tense and uncomfortable. He couldn't really fathom why she was here, or perhaps he didn't want to.

"Well, you've had a productive four years since the divorce."

She cleared her throat, "Yes, I've been busy."

"More than that, I should say." He poured some wine into a glass and put it before her. She smiled, so predictable. He didn't ask if she wanted it, just did it. But deliberately, she didn't touch it.

"Do you want some of these calamari? They're delicious."

She shook her head, "No, I hate that stuff."

"Really? That's funny. I don't remember that."

"I guess you weren't paying attention." She smiled without feeling.

Edward calmly sipped his red wine, very dry. She knew that without tasting it. He took small, controlled, measured sips.

It seemed an apt metaphor for his personality. He was measured and controlled, always in control of himself and his surroundings.

There had been a time, a long time ago, when she had thought such attributes to denote confidence, but now, from her vantage point, they spoke of something else altogether.

Hallie, think before you speak. Think about what impression you make — how it looks.

Where had they been? An office party? *Everything you do reflects on me.* **You are a reflection of me.**

Had he said it? She couldn't remember. It felt as though he did. He acted as though he had.

The waiter arrived with the menus and pulled her back to the present. "Can I bring you anything else while you—"

"Yes," Hallie cut him off abruptly, "I'd like a glass of white zinfandel."

He smiled, looking a little sheepishly at the glass of red wine already in front of her. "Of course, Ma'am." And then he was gone.

She found Edward eyeing her with some calculation, some interest. Evidently, she had surprised him. "So, Hallie, my secretary, read one or two of your books. I don't remember the titles. Are you going to continue writing the same sort of thing?"

Here it comes. That was Edward's code for he disapproved of her subject matter. She smiled again. Why she was finding this awfully amusing was beyond her. Perhaps she was just perverse. "Do you mean the vampire horror books?"

He whitened a bit around his mouth, "I suppose."

"Well, since you asked Edward, I was thinking about heading in another direction."

He nodded as he, perhaps a tad too gingerly, stuffed a piece of calamari in his mouth. "That might be a wise move on your part."

She nodded, "Do you think?"

"Well, for your own best interest, you don't want to be labeled as a particular sort of writer."

"No, you know. I think you're right. I've decided that my next book is going to have a lot more graphic sex in it. Sex and blood because it will be vampire sex."

She noted that Edward was now frowning when the waiter arrived. He placed Hallie's wine in front of her beside the untouched glass of red. She smiled prettily at him, then took a big noisy slurp out of it. The young dark-haired man just stared at her with somewhat astonished eyes and then hesitantly asked, "Are you ready to order?"

Edward began with steely control in his voice, "I think we need—"

"You know, I'd like some spaghetti and meatballs with great big meatballs." She turned to the waiter, "Are they pretty large?" And then she giggled, "You know the meatballs."

"Um, well, Ma'am, I can ask the chef to make the meatballs extra-large if you want."

She grinned, "That would be super."

"And for you, sir?"

The frown was still in place. "I'll have the eggplant parmesan."

He nodded, "Very good." And made a hasty retreat.

Hallie smiled with extra sparkle at Edward, "What do you want to talk about now?"

Jack was glad they couldn't hear him because he was sure he would bring down the walls of this place with the roars of his laughter.

Edward fiddled nervously with his wine glass as Hallie swirled her spaghetti artistically around her fork. The sauce on her spaghetti was thin and runny. A proper metaphor for the whole evening, she thought with perverse amusement. He'd scarcely spoken to her since their initial conversation. She remembered in the past when he'd use his silences as chastisements. But that was back when she gave a shit.

She was careful not to look directly at him too often. Certainly, she didn't want him to think she was too interested. Although she was, though not in the way he thought. He appeared and acted the same, but somehow, he seemed a weaker man, a bit less composed and less sure of himself. Or perhaps she was the one who had changed, and she just saw him through different eyes.

Even though her life felt mostly like a bit of a shamble just now, she was undeniably a stronger woman. Life had strengthened her metal. Loss and difficulty had placed steel in her spine. Whether that was better or not, it was a reality. To allow herself to be molded again by anyone would be impossible. Her core was too brittle. Her personality was set and fired by struggle.

As she sat across from Edward, calmly reflecting, there was no denying that it would be gratifying for her at this juncture to find more chinks in his armor. To find that all his selfishness and insensitivity had eroded him through the years, just as she had predicted.

Then, unexpectedly, an image of him from long ago she'd forgotten suddenly surfaced. It had been nearly a week after their baby had been stillborn. She was walking by the baby's nursery, which she had meticulously prepared for.

As she came to the doorway, she stopped. Edward was inside the room, sitting in the rocking chair she'd picked out not one month before. His face was in his hands, and he was hunched over.

She knew he was crying, something quite honestly, in all their years together, she couldn't remember Edward ever having done before. She knew that he could use her comfort. But there was nothing left inside her to comfort him with. She was empty, having only bitterness left to fill her. Her feelings for him had died long ago. The baby was only the last reason to stay.

The anger she still carried toward him softened at the memory. It had been easier to think of him as the great monster that pain had created in her mind instead of like this — just a person, weak, flawed, but not really a monster. All the failures with Edward, she had turned inward on herself. All of the pain and humiliation of those years began to ease just a bit.

She felt lighter, lighter of heart than she had for such a long time. Her fork slipped unceremoniously from her fingers and clanked onto the plate. Taking her napkin off her lap, she tossed it onto the table. "Well, Edward, much as this has been an eye-opening evening, I have a life, and it's time for me to go."

His eyebrow rose crookedly in surprise. "You're leaving?"

"Yes, I've had enough and want to go home."

"Hallie," he began cautiously, "There is something I've wanted to speak to you about all evening, but I've been hesitant."

"Well, that doesn't seem like you. As I remember, you never had much problem conveying your feelings."

He smiled grimly, "You dislike me a great deal now, don't you?"

She shrugged, not wanting to deny what had become obvious even to him in his obtuseness.

He cleared his throat, "Yes, well, I suppose you've always been more generous than I."

"I suppose I have," and then she added, "in the past."

"So, you'll indulge me for a few more minutes."

"Not necessarily," she quipped, more than eager to leave without hearing any confessions from him. It wasn't necessary. Anything that she'd wanted to find out, she had. He'd outlived his usefulness.

"This is difficult. You know me. I'm not a fanciful person. My life is grounded in the real world."

Her mind briefly flickered across the tall, dark-haired secretary that Edward had gotten in the sack while Hallie was pregnant.

It was the only one she knew of, although she suspected others. She wondered if that had been one of his more grounded moments. "Your point?"

"Lately, well honestly, lately I've been having feelings concerning you."

"Feelings?"

He adjusted his tie. He really was nervous. How odd and delightful. "Yes, thoughts, feelings, even some dreams."

"No kidding."

"I know you to be a more open sort of person than I am, open to strange things."

She grinned. He had no idea how strange. How would he respond now if she told him she'd fallen in love with a ghost? He'd probably take it as a confirmation of all his past condemnations of her. She said nothing, content to let him stew in his own anxiety.

"So, I was wondering. Do you think dreams mean anything?"

She considered carefully, feeling a trap nearby waiting for her to topple in. "No, I don't."

"Nothing at all?"

"No. I think they're merely a reflection of what you've had for dinner."

He blanched a bit, which was no easy feat considering his natural complexion. "I'm surprised." Did she note a disappointment in his voice? Did she care?

"Anything else?"

"I was just going to tell you about a dream that I had, but if you don't think it means anything."

"No, not a thing," she fired back quickly.

"Well, frankly, because I was very drawn to you in the dream and thought it might mean—" Then he stopped, and she was grateful.

"It means nothing, Edward. Don't overthink it. Let it go." She glanced up at him for a second. He seemed completely befuddled, as though the woman before him was a complete stranger. To him, perhaps she was.

"Then you're happy, apart, I mean?"

She picked up her purse. She couldn't wait to tear out of here. "Perfectly happy, Edward," she stood up. Goodbye, I have to run." And she forced her anxious feet to slow their pace out of the restaurant.

He watched her the rest of the evening, somewhat perplexed. Her thoughts were not with him. They were somewhere else. Slaying dragons of her own, he suspected.

He was gratified in some measure by the way the evening had gone with Edward but disturbed at the same time. Yes, he was jealous. Not of Edward as a man, from what he'd seen, he was pretty worthless, but of Edward as a living, breathing man existing in the same physical space as Hallie. That was something insurmountable that he could not compete with. But he couldn't deal with that reality at the moment. There was another matter.

Hallie pulled a light blue afghan that she had wrapped around her shoulders more tightly around her. It was perceptible. The cold spots in the house were growing. Edward's sudden appearance at this time was no coincidence. He was influenced. *It* was getting desperate to somehow pull her away from him. He was a threat. *It* was getting reckless, and that alarmed him greatly. Now, he struggled with the dilemma of whether or not it was the time to make Hallie aware of the other presence in the house.

She settled in the rocking chair with a tablet on which she was scribbling notes and slowly began to doze into a light sleep.

It was what he'd been waiting for. He closed his own eyes, intent on catching her in between.

Hallie's eyes flickered open. She was still in the den. Everything appeared the same except for one small thing. Jack was standing across the room near the fireplace. Funny, how natural it seemed to see him standing there. It hadn't startled her at all. "I must be dreaming," she whispered.

At the sound of her voice, he turned to her. He was dressed casually in a blue shirt and khaki pants. The blue shirt just emphasized the clear blueness of his eyes. He looked so absolutely gorgeous and vibrant to her. How could he not be alive? But he didn't seem happy. "You're somewhere in between. That place between dreaming and wakefulness."

She smiled, straightening up. "Why come here? We have such interesting dreams together."

He didn't seem amused or even enticed. Something definitely was bothering him. "It's safer this way."

"Safer? Why?"

He came near, sitting in the recliner next to her. Instinctively, she reached out to touch him, but he pulled back. "Better not. This is a very tenuous state."

"What's the matter? You look so grim."

He frowned more explicitly, "Did you enjoy your dinner?"

Ah, he seemed a little upset with her, perhaps about Edward. "Were you there?" She rubbed her eyes. It truly felt as though she was awake. Jack was so near. She swore she could feel the warmth emanating from him.

"I tag along at most places you go." She'd never seen him so out of sorts, even when he'd stood on his New York City balcony explaining that he was really a ghost.

"Well, the food wasn't very good, and the company was worse."

He nodded, "I was a little surprised you went at all."

She rubbed her arms. It was so chilly here now, and his intensity made her uncomfortable. He was possessive of her, for someone who wasn't even alive very possessive, or was it protective? "Yes, I was surprised too. I guess I had to prove some things to myself."

He rubbed his hands together thoughtfully. He had such nice hands, big, strong hands that looked like they could build a house or sculpt a great work of art. "Did you?"

She smiled sadly, "Who knows? Somehow, I think closure is a myth. But I feel better about things, some things." She looked away, struck again by the enormity of their particular dilemma.

He grimaced, not yet willing to let it go. "Edward has caused you a lot of pain in the past. I think it would be best for you to avoid him."

She smiled a little bemused. "Is that an order, Jack?"

"No, let's just say it's a deep desire of mine. It's my experience not to trust a snake once it's bitten you. And you're very trusting."

"I never said I trusted him, Jack. I just had to set some things straight in my own mind. Maybe prove I had changed," she paused, "at least to myself."

With a tangible sigh, "I understand."

"Do you?"

"No, but I'll put it aside if you say so." He had to admit he did feel a difference in her. It would not be perceptible to everyone, but there was a quality, a greater assurance. Much as he'd hated her going, perhaps she had gained something during her meeting with Edward. Maybe she wasn't as vulnerable as he thought she was. Grimly, he wondered if he was really someone she needed now. "It's not as though I can really have any kind of claim on you."

Now, she was getting disgruntled. "First of all, I'm not that trusting." He smiled at her. Evidently, he wasn't buying it, "second, I'll decide who has and hasn't a claim on me."

His eyebrow raised, "Really?"

"Yes, and I care about you," she tacked on, "a lot."

"I know that."

"Do you Jack? Do you have any idea how ridiculously tormenting this situation is?"

His eyes on her were unflinching. "Yes, Hallie, you're not the only tormented one." She looked away, wondering if she was blushing. The intonation of his voice reminded her of his kisses and the feel of his arms around her.

Another wave of palpable cold hit her, and she pulled the afghan tighter around her shoulders. Jack looked around almost angrily. "What is it, Jack?"

He shook his head. "It's complicated."

"Is there anything about this situation that isn't complicated?"

"I think you should push to finish your book. This house may not be the best place for you right now."

"Why? What is it?"

"I don't want to worry you, Hallie."

"Too late," she quipped.

Again, he looked at her intently. She knew and felt there was more he wasn't saying. "Can you just trust me for a little while, Hallie?"

She shrugged, dissatisfied, "I don't seem to have a lot of choice here."

He nodded, "There is something I need to ask you about, though."

"What is it?"

"It's about Sebastian Winters."

CHAPTER TWELVE

Samory

He patiently waited in the den for Hallie's Aunt Marie. Hallie had gone to bed hours ago. He had been beside her, watching her sleep. On some level, he supposed, he had delayed acting on this front. His purpose in being here had been clear to him for some time, although fully acknowledging it was another matter. He was to free Hallie from whatever this thing was that had insinuated itself into her life.

But in doing so, he also knew his reason for being here would no longer exist. Even contemplating not being with or near Hallie left him with a sense of intolerable hopelessness. This ongoing struggle had only been exacerbated by a recent awareness. An anxiousness had set in as though time was running out, and an inevitability was becoming clear.

A clock was ticking somewhere. There wasn't any more room for his selfishness. It was far past time to put himself behind her needs.

Aunt Marie stood in the shadows across the room, her expression grave. "I see you've gotten down to business."

"I need a few questions answered."

She moved toward him, looking somewhat different. A little younger, he thought. Her hair was blondish now and only sprinkled with gray. "What's happening with you?"

"I'm changing a bit to a younger version of myself. My time here, helping you is reaching its conclusion, and the physical self you see is reverting into a proper reflection of my spirit."

He nodded, "I don't really follow."

"I know," that warming grin, "but it's not very important right now. Let's just say it's the natural course of things. What do you want to know?"

As was his custom with Aunt Marie, directness seemed the best avenue. "I spoke to Hallie tonight. And she told me about her first inspiration for Sebastian Winters."

The smile turned grim, "Don't you mean appearance?" He could see she was on the same page, so to speak, as he was, "Yes, perhaps I do. She said that it was not long after her divorce from Edward."

"Yes, I remember that." Her voice became distant, as though she were flipping through a scrapbook from long ago. "She'd gone back to spend some time at her mother's house in North Carolina. Hallie was in very bad shape back then, Jack. I could venture to say the lowest point of her life. You see, she'd lost a baby earlier that year."

"Yes, and she said it was her intention just to begin writing her thoughts down when—when something guided her to begin the first Samory novel."

She clicked her tongue in agreement. It was a little affirmative noise that he'd noticed she was apt to do at odd moments. "Channeling."

"What was that?"

"Of course, it must be. When another spirit uses your body for its purposes, in this case for self-expression."

"A little grisly for self-expression."

She shrugged, "Well, I suppose you have to consider the source."

"So, then you're saying Sebastian Winters is actually—"

"That's right, my boy, someone else entirely."

"But that can't be right because I've seen Hallie writing, and much of it comes from her."

"Except the part that comes from you." Her eyes sparkled impishly. She hadn't missed anything. Maybe she had a point. Perhaps he wasn't the only influence here, and he had cut in on *Its* turf. No wonder it was so damn angry.

"I had the idea there might be some clue in that first piece that Hallie wrote."

"Maybe at least in the world she created."

"What do you mean the world?"

Her soft, light voice had taken on a steely quality. "What I mean to say is that I think you might need to take a little trip, Jack, into the reality of Sebastian Winters."

That elusive feeling of urgency swept up through him again. "That sounds a bit unsettling."

"Yes," she said solemnly, "I imagine it will be."

The house lay silenced by the darkness of the night. He had visited Hallie again. Silently, he watched her, so horribly tempted to throw caution to the wind and enter her dreams where she could be his. But he knew it was too risky. No matter how much the possibilities beckoned and tantalized him, he couldn't leave her unprotected again.

He left her under the guard of the hound bearing his name and headed into the study. There was work, *wild work*, to be done. He'd spotted it standing on her bookshelf amongst other volumes. It was in paperback. None of her books had made it into hardback. They'd gone straight to paper.

Her contributions to literature swirled in the genre of pulp fiction. But what did it matter? They had a following. They were moneymakers, and for some, they'd provided an avenue of temporary escape from the pressures and mundaneness of everyday existence. Who was to say that wasn't great success? And after all, he was very much in love with their author, at least one of them.

He picked it up, the one that had started it all. Holding the book in his hands, he turned it over with curiosity. The title remained unspoken on his lips — *Vengeance's Angel*. He had heard once that it was always an author's first work that was most autobiographical. But it wasn't Hallie's life he was interested in unearthing at this juncture.

Slowly, he perused the teaser on the back cover.

Out of the darkness rises a creature of vengeance. Less than a God but more than a man — part hero, part monster trapped beneath the confines of a curse, bidden to use his compelling, exotic appeal to wreak havoc on an unsuspecting modern world.

Ah, huh, he sighed deeply. Right now, he'd much rather have a look at the sports page. He did love Hallie, even if the stuff she wrote was a bit mucky. He settled down in a nearby chair and began thumbing through the novel, or novella.

It wasn't terribly long, just over a hundred or so pages. It began,

Samory walked in a separate reality, taking steps in the mortal world yet somehow apart from it, as though he were a phantom who occasionally donned flesh to hunt his prey.

Well, wasn't that wonderful? His memory of Hallie's creation still irritated him. He didn't care if he was a poor, misunderstood bastard of a vampire. The guy was a major pain in the ass to him. He skipped forward,

Samory did not allow himself to care about anyone. These creatures of the flesh were as a breed of animal beneath him that served a purpose. He did not let himself consider that they had dreams or hopes. They were nothing to him, and the memory of his life that had once been was like a distant impression that had perhaps been someone else's dream.

Yes, yes, enough of Samory's psychological dilemmas. We get the angst already. He skipped forward a few more pages.

"Samory," Samory heard his name whispered through the turbulent corridors of his mind. But he wouldn't allow himself to be touched or swayed by the sweet echoes of life. His heart was frozen to sentiment. The white throat that lay beneath his questing, passionate mouth would not be real to him, only the descendent

offspring of a black-hearted hypocrite. There would be no mercy to her. She could be nothing to him. All he could allow himself to do was follow the ancient call of hunger, of the life force of blood flowing through the woman's veins. His sharp white teeth bit mercilessly into flesh, and her screams—.

He shuddered. Lovely, nothing like a little gore to settle one's nerves. His eyes continued to scan somewhat distastefully further into the book. Who would have known Hallie had such violence inside her? Then again, he wondered whose violence it truly was.

The serving wench who bore the name Madeline McCormick was not an exceptional beauty. At least, he didn't think so. But there was something about the waitress in the greasy little diner that kept pulling Samory's focus back to her. What was it about this female? And then he recognized the resemblance, of course, the large green eyes that seemed to devour you with their need.

He paused. Now, this was of interest.

He remembered that look of hunger, a void so deep within her soul that she threatened to absorb your very essence. It was that horrible dichotomy of the unconscious predator. They were innocent in that they didn't know their need devoured and destroyed. It was this that he remembered from a distant past long forgotten. The eyes were on another face, only one of many paintings in a gallery of recollection.

He thought of Hallie's collection of acquaintances in the real world. After all, didn't real people inspire characters sometimes, or maybe not? Fiction had never been something he enjoyed reading too much. Except, of course, Agatha Christie, now there was a complex female.

Hallie's eyes certainly weren't so needy they devoured your soul, nor were Monica's. He supposed it might be Hallie's mother or sister. The snapshot he'd seen from Hallie's wallet flashed through his mind. Their eyes were certainly not like that.

A strong chill swept through the room. He looked around expectantly — the presence again. Could he be onto something here? What had Aunt Marie said about entering the reality Hallie had created in her books? Was that truly possible?

He closed his eyes and felt the coldness sweep around him. It almost felt welcoming now, which bothered him immensely. He hesitated. It seemed as though this journey might not be as difficult as he thought, but that, too, concerned him.

Red, bright, flashing warning lights were going off all around him. *It* was making all of this too damn easy. But where was the alternative?

It was imperative he find some answers for Hallie's sake. Jack returned to the written page. His concentration focused on the print. And then he went within. He willed himself to open, to feel the flood of energy behind the words. There was a current here, an undeniable pull. Around him, the room shifted, and this reality bent to make room for another.

It was another time. He could see Hallie hunched over a laptop computer, quietly but intently filling the screen with words. The waves of anguish he felt pouring from her were profound. But that wasn't all. He recognized it immediately. Something else was here, covering her, draping itself over her.

He couldn't see it, but it was as tangible as anything he'd ever touched. *It* was there, barring him from getting too close, encircling her, flooding, feeding her with its emotions. But *It* was not filled with anguish but instead with rage.

He had to go deeper. What were Aunt Marie's words? You must cloak yourself in another's reality, in the world she had created on the page. He opened himself further,

Samory watched the young woman with fascination. She still had her youth, but already it was showing signs of wear from the world.

Perhaps all of that raging need was devouring her from within. Would he bestow his gift to her to preserve at least her flesh? After all, he could see already that she, an instinctual predator, came to it naturally. And then she saw him, and he remembered the other he hadn't chosen to save.

Jack could feel the flood of emotion beneath the words like rippling tides threatening to overcome him. All he had to do was let go, and he would be there. But there was fear, a tangible fear pulling him the other way. He focused on Hallie, the feel of her, the animation of her eyes, and her strong but gentle spirit. Steeling himself, he consciously let go, allowing his spirit to totally be sucked into the dark world.

He awoke with dizziness, his head lying on a cold, stone floor. The air was damp, and his vision was unbelievably blurry. He breathed in and felt what could only be described as stale air entering his lungs. Pushing back the gagging reflex, he found that his eyes were gradually beginning to adjust. He tried to breathe shallowly so as not to inhale too much. Funny, in Hallie's house, he had never once had to concentrate on breathing.

In the darkened corners of the room, he could now perceive a movement scurrying around. A creepy feeling of disgust swept through him as vivid images of what was making that movement fluttered through his mind. Just wonderful, he straightened up with effort. There was a definite clammy, moldy smell in this place — one he didn't care to explore further.

He looked around, trying to quickly assess his environment. The entire room appeared to be made of stone—stone shelves and inscriptions on the stone walls. He stood up, his knees trembling, brushing himself off of the dustiness that seemed to have enveloped him.

As he moved closer to them, he could make out some dates chiseled on the walls — the 1800s, the latest, the 1920s, and names nearly unrecognizable with age. With reluctance, he began to acknowledge where he'd landed — a tomb of some kind, a mausoleum.

"Good to see you, old fellow. We've been expecting you." Jack regrettably recognized the voice and slowly turned to face its author. The always impressive figure walked out of the shadows. His face was pale against the black suit he wore — modern dress for a modern vampire. "My luck that I arrive after dusk."

"That's when all the action takes place, friend." His voice was deep but laced with his rich, foreign accent, no doubt a variation on Transylvanian.

"So, what is this, Samory? Your home away from home? I expected something a little more polished."

He laughed heartily, apparently amused by Jack's presence. "Yes, well, I imagine the idea of roughing it is foreign to you, Jack Brennan. It's just a little safe house that I have tucked away. You can't be too careful when you're me." And he added,

"You never know when pesky sea captains may be nosing around trying to make things complicated."

Jack smiled and laughed without sincerity, looking around for an escape hatch. What in the world was he going to do now? Aunt Marie hadn't prepared him for anything of this nature. "Well, Samory, who exactly is this we you referred to?"

He smiled malevolently with his chalky white teeth, "Why myself and my creator."

"You mean Hallie?"

"Don't be coy, Mr. Brennan. I know why you're here, to cause more trouble."

"Trouble? What kind of trouble could I cause for you? You're the man in these books, aren't you? If you went, so would Hallie's career," he coughed a bit. The dustiness around him seemed to have crept directly into his throat.

Samory's already black eyes appeared to darken. "One would think so. But since you've arrived, Mr. Brennan, you've displaced me in Hallie's affections and then, with no gallantry or sense of fair play, have attempted to rip Gabriella from me with that dolt of a creation of yours."

"I wouldn't be so hard on the Captain if I were you. He seems to be making some progress," he laughed and then stopped when he noted Samory's scowl.

"He's an imbecile."

"Well, be that as it may," again, looking around, trying to lock onto the entrance to the tomb, "I'll put in a good word for you when I get back."

"You're assuming a lot. Hallie has just fallen under your influence temporarily."

"As opposed to your influence."

He smiled grimly, "I have always been just a player."

"Is that so?" He glanced around apprehensively, "Then who pulls the strings around here?"

"You don't really think we're going to let you out of here, do you?"

Jack felt his energy waning. He was unnaturally tired, a tightness in his chest. He was wondering if being here was draining something out of him. He leaned against one of the granite walls, not wanting to consider whom he was cozying up to. He had to be subtler. A full frontal attack was not working. "Well," he cleared his throat again of dust, "Samory, there's no reason for us to get nasty. You must be a lonely guy. I mean, loner that you are."

The vampire laughed without humor, "What's your point?"

"I thought we could talk. Tell me about yourself, about your past. I hate to admit I haven't been an avid reader of Hallie's books. Maybe you could fill in the blanks."

The charismatic Nosferatu looked suspicious. "What are you up to, Brennan?"

"When you were one of us, I mean not like me. A human, wasn't there someone special?"

"That was eons ago."

"Yes, but you never forget that first love. Do you, big guy?"

He looked displeased, "The past is a cold place."

"Can't be much worse than here."

Samory's eyes almost seemed to glaze a bit, and Hallie's character looked as if he was momentarily pulled back into the narrative. His voice became filled with gothic melodrama. "There was a time," he began.

"Yes, long ago," Jack prodded.

"It was so long ago. I was a king, and she was a mere country maiden in the village. An innocent, filled with such goodness, but I was a king. And she was unworthy. So, I let my love for her become twisted and—"

He waited impatiently, the tightness in his chest becoming a crushing pain. It was all too evident now that he couldn't exist on this plane for very long. "And what? What happened? You destroyed her?"

"No, I was damned by her to this eternal life of suffering."

"Really?" His vision was beginning to swirl. He couldn't guess the rules here, but it felt like time was running out.

And then Samory's eyes widened with what Jack could only interpret as fear. He'd slipped. Jack could feel it. Maybe it was a key of some sort. "What happened to the maiden, Samory?"

"No more," his voice was deep but edged with panic.

"How could she damn you? Was she a witch, an enchantress," silence, "or did she just create you?"

"Noooo," the voice boomed from the mausoleum and seemed to resonate from everywhere.

And then Jack felt himself hurled, actually physically expelled, from where he was. He tumbled face-first into a small patch of grass.

His bruised body rested on the moist earth. For quite some time, he was reluctant to move. He'd forgotten what pain felt like. But shortly after, once his skin began to tingle and then itch, he reassessed. Awkwardly pulling himself up on his knees, it felt as though every part of him was battered. He drew in a deep, cool breath that, thankfully, was not dusty.

Around him, he recognized the shapes in the darkness — statues and tombs. Evidently, it seemed that Samory had managed to thrust him just out of the mausoleum. The dynamics of Hallie's world eluded him, but he was no fool. He stood up, still feeling shaky. At least that crushing pressure in his chest had left. That was something. With effort, he started to make his way toward the cemetery gates. He didn't want to be around when Samory thought better of his rash reaction.

The city, Hallie's city, in darkness, reminded him somewhat of a mix between Chicago and New Orleans. He gathered that Hallie didn't have a firm setting in mind. As he wandered amidst a largely abandoned urban area, he wished he'd read the book more carefully or at least once through. At least, then, maybe he would have a sense of where everything, or anything, was located. It was chilly and foggy, and his stomach ached with hunger. Now, there was a sensation he hadn't felt for some time. He spotted the coffee shop across the dimly lit street. Actually, it was the only building around that looked marginally active.

What was it he'd read about that coffee shop? There was some waitress that Samory was giving the eye. Well, with luck, he could grab a bite to eat and get out before the old boy made an appearance. With luck, he grimaced. Was that possible in this universe? He stepped onto the street artistically lined on the edge with cobbled brick. As he made his way to the entrance, he felt a coolness touch his skin and a haziness in his vision as though he had just passed through a patch of fog. More atmosphere on Hallie's part, he concluded rather dismally.

He swung the glass double-door entranceway of The Coffee Pot open. This, he suspected, was the greasy spoon that, for some reason, Hallie had made pivotal in her first novel. Overcome by the pressing demands of physical life, he'd forgotten, for a moment, the whole reason for his fantastical journey — to collect information. He was here to find a way to resist the presence intent on dominating Hallie's existence. He sat down at a very small table situated near the window so that he could strategically mark anyone's approach.

He hadn't thought to feel his pockets to see if he'd been supplied with any currency in this existence. It didn't much matter at this moment. He planned to make a run for it sooner or later anyway. He strummed his fingers on the flimsy metal table, wondering distractedly how Hallie was doing back in Virginia.

It was novel being here, having a conventional body again, but there was also an oppressiveness. The atmosphere of everything he saw and touched was laced with a depressive heaviness. No happy, light-hearted inhabitants around here.

More than anything, he wished he was back with Hallie. But he couldn't return empty-handed. He had to accomplish something while he was here, even just a little something.

"What can I get you, sir?" He looked up, startled, into a pair of enormous green eyes. Distracted by his thoughts, he'd forgotten for a moment to keep watch. Oh yeah, this must be

Samory's serving wench. What was her name? The big-name tag glared back at him in bold letters — *Madeline*.

The sharply boned face frowned at him. "I got customers. Do you want to order?" He smiled. Her accent was clipped somehow, almost Bronx-like. So far, there was a mix of New York, Chicago, and New Orleans—must be all of Hallie's favorite cities.

After all, anything was possible in fiction. "Look, mister, Sal doesn't cater to loiterers. Either order or hit the road." He could certainly see why Samory was drawn to her. Evidently, he liked a woman with a bad attitude.

"I haven't seen a menu."

"Sal," she yelled toward the kitchen. "This one needs a menu."

And then he heard a disembodied voice boom back, "Well, why don't he go to the tearoom down the street?"

She turned back to him with a very sour expression, "Sal said—"

"Yeah," he interrupted, "I heard. Well, how about a cheeseburger, fries, and a chocolate milkshake." He might as well indulge.

She scribbled it down and placed one hand strategically on her hip to indicate a mix of femininity and authority. He'd recognized the confrontational stance. He'd seen it with plenty of business associates and other female acquaintances.

"It will just be a few," she quipped, and then was gone.

He watched as she disappeared into the swinging doors that evidently led into Sal's domain. She was a strange creature. She acted like a stereotypical waitress, but there was an odd feeling, something out of place. Maybe it was as Samory had described — her predatory eyes. Or maybe the gloominess of the atmosphere was causing him to suspect everything and everyone.

He leaned back in the uncomfortable metal chair and closed his eyes for a minute. He was tired, unbelievably tired. This little jaunt was sapping quite a bit of energy out of him.

He thought about Hallie, her smile, her laugh, what it was like to kiss her.

The front doors of the coffee shop swung open. Damn it, he had to stay focused. At this rate, he would have everyone sneak up on him. He braced himself for a confrontation with Samory, but it wasn't Samory who crossed the threshold. The face that greeted him was not unfamiliar, nor was it welcome.

Edward, Hallie's Edward, stepped into the coffee shop, dressed to the tee in a navy-blue business suit with a briefcase in hand. His eyes swept through the room, and then he focused on Jack and looked at him with anticipation.

CHAPTER THIRTEEN

Madeline

Edward's eyes stared at him, wide with expectancy, although the rest of his pallid face remained unanimated. Then again, Jack had reason to believe this was his status quo. Jack looked all around, even behind him, hoping Edward's attention was focused elsewhere.

But as was his luck, and or lack of it in this universe, he was the target.

He stopped in front of Jack's rickety two-seater metal table. Edward stretched out a long, pale hand toward him. "I believe you've been expecting me."

His eyes widened. He really wished he'd taken more time with that book. Caught in confusion as to how to respond, Jack returned Edward's flaccid grip, "Uh no, not really."

The hand was withdrawn. "Then, you aren't Mr. Samory Delacroix."

Jack frowned. Evidently, his nemesis was expected here tonight. "No, 'fraid not."

Edward's thin lips turned down in a perturbed expression Jack had seen more than once in their limited acquaintance. "I see." Jack frowned, but Edward wasn't taking the hint. He just stood there dumbly in front of him. "We had an appointment."

Jack nodded in acknowledgment. "Well, he's not here." Apparently, Hallie hadn't made Edward's character too swift. No big surprise there, given their history.

Again, Edward muttered, "I see."

Jack glanced back toward the kitchen. Where was Madeline with his cheeseburger? Edward looked down in befuddlement at his watch. "I suppose I might be a little early. Perhaps I should wait."

Jack shrugged at him. Something was odd. It was almost as if his presence here in Hallie's book had thrown the other characters off. Edward looked at him pointedly. "What do you think? Should I wait?"

Jack considered carefully. He hadn't read far enough in the novel to absorb the plot details, much less Edward's presence here. But knowing Hallie's feelings toward her ex-husband at that point of her life in which she penned the novel, and the fact that he was meeting Samory. In Jack's estimation, all of this boded ill fortune for the scrawny ex-husband. The tantalizing enigma was whether he bought Edward a little extra time or threw him into the clutches of—"Yeah, sure, why don't you wait."

Edward nodded, "Ah, well, do you mind if I join you?"

By the time Jack opened his mouth to reply, the squirrelly guy was sitting at the tiny table across from him. Pushy fellow — again, he wondered what Hallie could have seen in him. "My name is Lester Canon, I'm an attorney." Lester, nice name, Hallie.

Evidently, she didn't hold attorneys in very high regard. Then again, he thought indulgently, she wrote this long before they'd met. "Oh." He tried hard not to encourage too much conversation.

"I, um, didn't catch your name, sir."

By then, Madeline had noiselessly sauntered up to their table, "What will you have, sir?" Edward, or rather Lester's eyes, got markedly round at her intrusion. Jack was beginning to think this was his only mode of expression.

"Better order, Lester. She'll kick your ass if you don't."

Madeline's eyes turned on him with a smoldering expression he couldn't quite pinpoint — some mixture of admiration and animosity.

Lester stammered out, "How about a cup of coffee?"

She smiled with no expression. "How about it?" And then she turned to Jack, "Your burger will be right up." Again, she was gone.

Lester's nose twitched a bit. "Abrasive, isn't she?"

Jack glanced out the front window of the coffee shop, but no sign of Samory yet. But then the fellow could approach quietly in a patch of fog or as a bat or a dog, no wolf. He wasn't too sharp on his vampire lore. Maybe he could still eat and get out before he arrived. But then he'd miss the events unfolding with

Lester here. Hmm, quite a dilemma. "So, Lester, what exactly are you meeting Samory about?"

"Samory, then you know Mr. Delacroix?"

Oops, "Just vaguely."

"Ahh, he contacted me about handling some of his business affairs, but strangely enough, he insisted on meeting me only after dusk and here in this coffee shop rather than in my office." He fidgeted a bit in the metal chair. Jack wondered distantly if he should be feeling sorry for the guy.

"So that's unusual?" Good grief, this was awkward. "For someone to have such requirements?"

Again, an Edward/Lester frown. "A bit."

"So, why did you accept?"

"I need the money."

"Well, that's valid." He commented and then allowed the confused silence to envelope them.

Madeline arrived at their side with a tray of food. Jack, for the first time, noticed that he and Lester were the only ones left in the restaurant. Apparently, the other customers had slipped out or just plain disappeared when he wasn't paying attention. She put the coffee cup down in front of Lester. "You want cream or sugar with that?"

"No, I take it black." Of course, he did. He wouldn't want it to taste like anything.

"And here's your cheeseburger and milkshake." She put the steaming plate and frosty glass down in front of Jack. He had to admit that regardless of where he was, this looked good.

And then he noticed Lester across from him wrinkling his nose in distaste.

"Do you have any idea the damage that meal could do to your arteries?"

"Well, Lester, I think I'll take my chances." He was beginning to wish Samory would hurry up and come and deal with this fellow so he could eat in peace.

"Anything else for you gentlemen?" Hand on the hip again and huge green eyes surveying them critically.

"No, that'll do," Jack smiled at her with little impact.

"Okay, because I'll be taking a break over there," she indicated a booth in the corner, "and having a cigarette."

"We'll call if we need you," Lester muttered nervously. She flipped a loose strand of brown hair behind her shoulders and glared with a note of irritation at Lester. "No, I'll be on a break," adding with emphasis, "having a cigarette." She took the little pad out of her pocket, ripped what Jack assumed was the bill off, and flicked it onto the table. "That's your ticket."

And then she turned on her heel, heading with drama towards a back booth. Did everyone in Hallie's books have an attitude?

"The service here is deplorable. I can't imagine why Mr. Delacroix insisted on meeting here."

"Maybe he likes the scenery." Jack took a big bite of his cheeseburger. It was a little greasy but not bad. And the milkshake was top-notch, and it actually froze his tongue. He had to take his hat off to Sal if he ever made an appearance.

A definitive chill swept through the untidy little restaurant. Disturbingly, Jack felt it sweep up his spine. Just like Samory to ruin the best meal he'd had in, well, a very long time.

A darkness seemed to gather outside the glass doors, and then they parted as Samory sort of silently whooshed in.

His dark eyes immediately fixed on Jack as he was lifting a French fry to his mouth.

"Is that Mr. Delacroix?" Lester uttered with trepidation.

"Yep," Jack muttered.

Samory moved toward them, his face reflecting at the least irritation. "Did you really think you could escape from me here, Brennan?"

"Not really, I was hungry."

"We hadn't finished our conversation."

Jack noticed that the already pale Lester seemed a shade lighter. "Careful, Samory, you'll intimidate the bit players."

His eyes then focused on Jack's squeamish companion. He smiled and bared his disturbingly white teeth. "You must be Mr. Canon. We had an appointment."

Lester looked as though he were ready to bolt out the door. "Yes, you're late."

"Forgive me, I was unavoidably detained." He delivered this smoothly and enigmatically, like a good vampire.

Jack picked up his burger and took another big bite. Not even in the face of these enormously extenuating circumstances did he want a bit of it to go to waste. "Too bad you can't enjoy this Samory. Sal makes a great burger."

"Enough of this, Brennan. It is time for you to leave."

"Can't do that, Samory. I haven't even paid Madeline over there." Jack noticed the puff of smoke emanating from the booth at the back of the restaurant.

At the mention of her name, Samory's eyes swept back in her direction with what Jack could only interpret as hesitation. "Maybe you and Lester should conduct your business while I finish up."

Lester stood up, looking at his watch. "It's really getting late. I have to get going."

"Now, Samory, how will that affect things if Lester here just gets up and leaves? Won't that make a page-turner?"

His dark eyes narrowed, "I'll deal with you later, Brennan."

"I look forward to it." Damn, it felt good to be in the driver's seat with this clown.

Samory concentrated what Jack surmised was his vampiric, hypnotic power on Lester and simply uttered the word, "Come."

Lester's eyes widened again, and his mouth hung open as he followed Samory outside. He really should feel sorry for the guy, but he certainly made it difficult. The pressure had returned again to his chest, coupled with the overwhelming fatigue.

He could only assume it had something to do with Samory. He knew it was time to find a way out of here, but how? His eyes focused on the trails of smoke coming from the booth in the back corner. In this crazy scenario, she was the one element that intrigued him. Somehow, he found her out of sync. Although why that was exactly, he couldn't put his finger on.

He quietly headed to the back of the restaurant and stood beside the booth where the waitress was languorously having her cigarette. She didn't look up at his approach, just stretched out a long almost bony arm and flicked the ashes in a beaten-up metal ashtray before her. This was a hard woman, one who'd been around. Not guileless like Hallie and not self-absorbed like Monica, but one who'd been toughened by life. So, what was she doing in Hallie's story?

"I wanted to give my compliments for the burger," he commented with caution.

"Sal will be delighted," but she didn't look up, just took a long draft of her shortening cigarette. "Would you like to join me, Jack?"

The back of his neck tingled with a scratchy prickling. He didn't remember giving her his name. "How did you know my name?"

She turned to him with green eyes wide and filled with shadows, "Word gets around. Have a seat." He slid into the booth across from her, feeling oddly like he'd just stumbled onto a nest of snakes. "Want a cigarette, Jack?"

She indicated the pack on the table in front of her. Though he desperately wanted one, taking it from her seemed oddly unwise. "No thanks."

"Suit yourself." She smiled vaguely, eying him with coolness. "Kind of bold of you to come here, considering what could happen."

He wasn't exactly sure what they were talking about, but it felt distantly like a threat. "I felt it was warranted."

"Maybe," she clicked her unkept nails on the table. "Maybe not, but I can see you're tenacious."

To him, it seemed like a strange word to come out of the mouth of this particular character. "Yes, when it's important, I am."

She smiled, "When it's important, we all are." She finished her cigarette and snuffed it out. "I think we could be friends, Jack. Why don't you get out of here before Samory comes back?"

A chill swept through him, and then an elusive sense of familiarity. "Are you?" he uttered, not exactly knowing what he wanted to ask.

"Better get going, Jack. Before it's too late."

He got up, almost not of his own volition. And then there was a tremendous push behind him, thrusting him through the kitchen's double doors.

He landed, none too softly, crashing onto the hard, aging linoleum of Hallie's kitchen. Thankfully, though painfully, he'd been ejected from that reality. As he pulled himself up shakily, memories began to tumble back somewhat broken. He stood there momentarily in the middle of Hallie's kitchen, breathing deeply.

It was there. Something had changed. He knew something now. For an instant, everything around him seemed to stop as all the pieces melded together before his eyes — the rage, the cold, the jaded and bitter eyes. How stupid he'd been, of course.

He'd had her right there and let her slip through his fingers. He closed his eyes, and the vision of Madeline's cold face rose in his mind. There she was, but now the large green eyes were filled unmistakably with hate. He'd found Sebastian Winters. Of that, he was convinced. He was a she and could not hide from him anymore.

CHAPTER FOURTEEN

The Cave

Hallie sat up in her bed, awakened suddenly from a restless sleep. She was anxious. Something felt very wrong. The digital clock glowed back three a.m. from the nightstand. Her eyes nervously swept the darkened room. Nothing was there, but that, too, wasn't right. It felt as though something was. "Jack," she whispered loudly into the semi-darkness, hopeful for a response but not really expecting one. For moments, nothing greeted her but stillness. And then the shadows shifted for an instant, and there was movement, movement from the darkness.

She clutched the covers tightly in her hands. Maybe this was that in-between state he'd found her in earlier in the evening. But it didn't feel the same. Then, she felt peaceful. Now, she was nervous, apprehensive. Jack had never had that effect on her before.

Again, as her eyes became more accustomed to the limited light, it seemed she could almost make out a form in the corner of the room. But it was indefinite.

Maybe it was her anxious imagination. Her heart was picking up its beat, now clearly with fear. Shakily, she spoke out, "Jack, if it's you, come out. You're scaring me."

And then, after what seemed like an endless stretch of time, there was another flicker of movement. She waited, barely breathing it seemed. Slowly, the form stepped partially into the light so that she could make out a face. She gasped instinctively, shocked at the stark vision before her.

It was a woman, but unlike any she'd ever encountered. The apparition stood about her height or a little smaller. Her face was beyond pale, almost as white as the sheet on her bed. And she seemed so unbearably thin, drawn-looking. Hallie was paralyzed. She felt as though she was breathing in gulps of fear. She couldn't be real. The only thing remotely alive about her was her eyes. Staring quietly back, they were enormous, a strange, almost unnatural, shade of green. A decrepit-looking nightgown of some sort hung on her. It was a faded blue, tattered looking, and loosely fit as though it were several sizes too large.

No, this couldn't be real. It must be a nightmare.

"Who are you?" Hallie managed to barely get out.

The voice that answered was calm and disturbingly empty of emotion. "Don't be afraid, Hallie."

Again, she asked, her voice trembling with controlled panic, "Who are you?"

And then the woman smiled, with almost a grimace that stretched across the width of her face but left her eyes untouched by any animation. "Can't you guess?"

Hallie shook her head, looking around the room for her dog, but even he was gone. She was completely alone.

"It's all right. I'm a friend of Jack's. I've come to take you to him."

"Jack? He sent you?" A slight glimmer of hope cracked through the veil of anxiety. "Why didn't he come himself?"

"He wanted to. But he was tied up with other things. He's trying to work it out so you can be together."

She was shivering beneath the thin sheet covering her. It felt drafty, so cold in the room. "Is that possible?" She whispered.

The woman shrugged her sharp, bony shoulders. "I've found in my experience that many things are possible, many, many things." As she moved closer, Hallie felt a familiar chill traverse her spine. She knew she'd never seen this woman before, but it felt as though there was something she should remember about her.

"Do I know you?"

Something flashed in the green eyes, but Hallie couldn't read her face. It was almost like a mask. She didn't let herself think about it too much, but it was logical that to be a friend of Jack's, you must be some kind of ghost. "No, you don't know me, Hallie, but I've watched you. I'm very proud of the work you've done."

"Proud? What do you mean?"

"Your writing has been good for women, all kinds of women who feel—" and there was a detectable hesitation, "weak."

She was shivering again. It was so cold. She struggled to control it. "I don't really understand."

"No, you've come away from that emotion. Haven't you? You've moved so far away."

She was beginning to feel very uncomfortable. Even beyond her intensely disturbing appearance, there was something extremely wrong about this person. "I just want you to tell me where Jack is."

Now, her eyes seemed to narrow. "So, now you're telling me what to do, are you?"

"No," she was too vulnerable here. She couldn't afford to enrage her, whatever she was. "No, I'm just worried about Jack."

"Yes, how we wrap our lives around men and forget everything we've accomplished. Isn't that always the way?"

"Please, just tell me where he is."

"I'll do better than that," and then she reached out an almost emaciated-looking hand toward her. "I'll take you to him."

An instinctual revulsion gripped Hallie. "I don't know you. I can't just go with you."

"But Jack needs you. He's hurt."

Panic and suspicion set in simultaneously. "He's hurt? How can he—"

"There are many things about living on this side you don't understand. He's given everything to help you, but now he needs your help," and then she paused. "Are you going to let him down, Hallie?"

She was breathing deeply. It was almost painful just now. What was wrong with her? Jack, what was going on? It was foolish, but how could she take a chance? "All right, I'll go."

No smile, no emotion, just— "Good, good girl, take my hand. It's not far where we're going. I've never been very far."

And when she touched the outstretched hand, Hallie felt the chill from the strange woman's flesh pass into her, into her blood.

And she was overtaken with dizziness. Distantly, a voice told her, "It's all right, just sleep now."

Jack walked into the den of Hallie's house, intent on finding Aunt Marie. He was excited but panicked at the same time. He kept feeling a mounting urgency as though time were of the essence. The woman, Madeline, or whoever the hell she was, would not be standing idly by. He was certain of this. After all, hadn't she planned for him to be sucked up into that universe of Sebastian Winter's as a somewhat permanent fixture? But fortunately for him, she'd miscalculated again.

When he reached the threshold of the den, something made him stop. It was a feeling. Something was wrong here. A tangible uneasiness had gripped him. And then he heard a scuffling noise behind Hallie's recliner. Tentatively, he moved closer, somewhat reluctant to find out what was there.

Bracing himself, he sprung quickly around the side of the chair. On the other side was a fur ball, huddling and trembling uncontrollably.

"Jack Jr.?" he whispered. The puppy seemed to sense his presence because his head popped furtively out from its hiding stance. Jack knelt down beside him. "What is it, boy?" He could feel waves of anxiety emanating from the little bundle. And then the realization came, and a knife of cold fear sliced through him, "Good God, where's Hallie?"

He jumped up, willing himself toward her bedroom as fast as he could. From the doorway, he saw her asleep on the bed, quietly, peacefully. He could see her chest moving in sleep, but as he moved closer, he knew all was not as it seemed. He felt the difference. Something was devastatingly wrong.

Beside him, he suddenly sensed the warm presence of Aunt Marie. "Something's wrong with her," he whispered with panic.

She nodded, her face as solemn and concerned as he'd ever seen it. "We made a mistake, Jack."

"What's happened? Tell me what has happened." He was in an absolute panic.

"She wasn't trying to get rid of you, just get you out of the way. So, she could do this."

Helplessly, he demanded, "What has she done?"

"Can't you feel it, Jack?"

He looked again at the quiet form whose breathing was still regular. And then he saw it, with his own eyes, and was horrified. There was no aura of life energy around her. Everything that made Hallie what she was had gone. What remained there lying on the bed was just a shell. "Her spirit, her spirit is gone!"

"Madeline led her away, and now she can't get back."

"Why? Why would she do that?"

"She evidently wants you to follow her somewhere, Jack. Somewhere where she feels secure."

His voice was filled with the fear coursing through him. "How do I get there?"

He looked to the older woman but received no answers, just eyes filled with boundless compassion.

He wandered aimlessly around the house, lost, helpless. Aunt Marie had left him alone with her strength, her prayers, and her blessing. That all felt useless to him now when all he needed was something concrete — a lead, some clue as to where Madeline had taken Hallie. He didn't even really know who or what Madeline was. Maybe she was some entity that had locked onto Hallie during the lowest point of her life like a parasite — one that was evidently willing to fight with a death grip to hold onto the connection. But where, where did that get him?

He sat in Hallie's favorite rocking chair and inhaled her scent from the afghan she always pulled around her.

Jack Jr. was below him, sniffing at his feet, looking as hopeless and bewildered as he felt. His head dropped, and he closed his eyes, trying desperately to focus on her but unable to get a strong feeling of her anywhere. And then, in his despair, he remembered something from the other life. It was a young boy all alone in his room, just praying for a little more time with the father who had just died — to hug him one more time and laugh with him just once more. All the prayers had gone unanswered, and all his life, he'd never asked for anything else until now.

He bowed his head and asked, with everything that was in him — asked desperately for help. He breathed deeply in stillness for a time that felt immeasurable to him. And then, finally, it felt as though the very air around him shifted a bit. There was a glimmer. He felt something — a perceptible warming around his heart area. His eyes opened, and his gaze was drawn to the fireplace's mantelpiece. There was something shiny up there he hadn't noticed or maybe hadn't been there before. He moved toward it. Of course, it was Hallie's heart necklace that her Aunt Marie had given her. It was so precious to her.

Grasping it in his hand, he felt the sweet, blissful feeling of her rush through him, the glow that emanated from her. It felt so good, so filled with love. He closed his eyes and felt a strong, steady pull back to the study. There was something there now. He was sure of it—something he hadn't seen before.

It had been there all the time. Of that, he was certain now. Somehow, it had been shielded from his sight, or perhaps he had never been able to see clearly without ego or prejudice before — the weapons that blind one to the truth. But he was ready to face the truth now, more for Hallie than himself. He was ready to let go of the self-deceptive illusions that had been part of him, part of the life that was before and that had been slowly stripped away one by one during his time here. There was simply no choice. Another came first now, and he could not afford to cling to what had been.

A large gaping hole was on the far side of Hallie's study. It pulsated not with life but with a chill, a dark frozenness that permeated its jagged entrance. This was where Madeline lived. She was the thing that clung so tightly that it would destroy rather than let go. And somewhere in that dark place was Hallie, too.

He moved closer to it. The opening reached the ceiling but was cut unevenly as though haphazardly ripped out of rock. It looked like something out of mythology — perhaps the entrance into an underworld.

He stood on its threshold, breathing its iciness deep into his lungs. Lord knows he didn't want to go in there. It was dark. It was cold. It was the stuff of nightmares. He would have preferred immensely to face Samory anytime, anywhere, in a fight, a duel, in the boxing ring. But who he was going to meet wasn't Samory. At least it couldn't kill him again. But that knowledge in itself was not comforting. One thing that he did feel now clearly standing here was that it was afraid — that was why she never ventured very far from her dwelling.

He stepped forward into the darkness. The chill wrapped around him—penetrating and arctic. He moved forward, actually hearing the crunch of ice beneath his steps. Reaching out to maintain balance, his hands touched the slick, frozen surface of the walls. What the hell was this? Why was it so unbelievably cold?

He literally forced himself to push on through the frozen tunnel. Ahead of him distantly, he could make out the wavering signs of light. He continued through the uneven portal, feeling the clamminess of the cave soaking into him. All he could do was concentrate on the light ahead of him. He moved on, although only dread filled him. For Hallie, for Hallie, he continued to chant in his mind like a mantra. She was the only reason he could press on.

The fear was so thick and tangible around him that it actually felt like a weight pressing on his body. Then, finally, after what seemed like an endless time, he reached the end of the black cave and stepped into something that he had not expected, not at all.

CHAPTER FIFTEEN

Temptation

Only flickering candles, dark red candles randomly placed throughout, lit the room. It was still cold here. In fact, there was frost on every piece of furniture. All the chairs and fixtures seemed worn down, as though they were very old but still recognizable. He was stunned, trying to wrap his mind around what he was looking at. Undeniably, it was a warped, worn down, frozen version, but there was no doubt about where he was.

He was in Hallie's study, some kind of hellacious, convoluted version of Hallie's study. It appeared there was no electricity with the exception of one place. The computer terminal was lit, the screen flashing on and off sporadically, but it did work. And there was someone there at it typing away frenzied, but it wasn't Hallie. And it certainly wasn't Samory. It was someone else.

The slight figure turned around to face him. Her face was emaciated, but her eyes were enormous, dark green eyes — the eyes of envy and jealousy. It was Madeline from the restaurant, sort of. He had to admit that Hallie's fiction had been much kinder in its portrayal. She was haggard-looking, almost skeletal, clutching a blanket tightly around her shoulders — obviously not untouched by the cold of her environment. Just beyond her, in the far corner of the dimly lit study in the gold wingback chair, was Hallie curled up, quietly sleeping. He moved toward her.

The wraith spoke, "I wouldn't do that, Jack. Disturbing her right now might be sort of dangerous." She grinned, obviously enjoying his distress. Even her gums were an unhealthy, faded, pink color.

"So, it's still Madeline, I presume."

Again, the smile stretched uncomfortably across her bony face. "Very good, but my friends call me Maddie."

He hesitated, "Sounds appropriate."

"So, what's it going to be? Are we going to be friends, Jack?"

Did her voice sound like a cackle when she talked, or was it just the influence of the atmosphere overtaking him?

He paused, a little surprised at the warmth of her cold greeting. His eyes quickly scanned the dismal surroundings. There didn't seem to be much he could do at the moment. So, he decided to humor the nutcase for a little while, while he devised a plan.

He grabbed an old, moldy-looking metal chair and turned it backward. Sitting down on it, he spoke in the most jovial manner he could muster. "I don't know, Maddie. What did you have in mind?" He smiled at the strange, emaciated woman in her decrepit nightgown, wondering for a moment what exactly the perks of this were for her.

She pulled the blanket a little closer around her, leaning against the decaying version of Hallie's computer desk. "Well, Jack, you don't mind if I call you Jack, do you?"

"Not at all. It seems we've been occupying a common space for some time."

Anger flared for a moment across her pale face, then was gone. Obviously, things weren't as cope septic between them as she'd like him to believe.

"I've brought you here for a reason. I want to make a deal."

He cleared his throat, "A deal?"

"Come to an understanding that will mutually benefit us."

"Really? I wasn't aware there was any common ground between us. You've been quite antagonistic in the past, Maddie. What makes you think we can work something out now?"

Anger again, good, good, keep the crazy woman off-balance. "Sometimes concessions have to be made."

He could read it clearly on her bony, little face. Apparently, something had changed. It flashed through his mind that it might have been Hallie's confrontation with Edward. She had moved so far beyond any need for Madeline that desperate measures had to be taken now.

"Is that what you've been doing, hiding out here, making concessions?"

Her expression grew hard, not that any of her expressions were particularly soft. "What do you mean?"

"Well, I just have to ask. Is all of this really worth hanging onto? No offense, Maddie, your place here isn't many steps up from a rat hole. And I don't know what you looked like before, but I've got to say you look like complete hell now."

"These are all superficial things." And then the green eyes narrowed. "You've always liked your comfort Jack, your pretty women. I'm a little surprised you didn't go for Monica. The package, shall we say, is a lot glossier."

Now, he frowned. This little conversation was beginning to irritate him. "Let's say my priorities have changed since I've been here."

"Oh yes, I've seen how selfless and noble you've become, even willing to face Samory on Hallie's behalf."

"Samory was a piece of cake."

"Samory is a puppet," she emphasized with a gesture of her particularly long and bony hand. "My puppet."

"Is that what Hallie is to you, Madeline?"

She stood up and walked away from him, her thin shoulders shaking with what he guessed might be rage. "I gave Hallie a reason to live when she had none. I gave her Sebastian Winters, a career, an identity from the wreckage that some man had caused."

"You mean Edward."

"Edward, Richard, Jack, any man, they're all selfish. They take everything and then leave you with nothing."

He swallowed and said quietly, "I'm not doing that to Hallie."

She whirled around to face him, her eyes blazing with hatred. "You're already doing it. She only thinks of you. She's destroying Samory for that idiot of a character you created. If you were together, what would you do, Jack? You'd eat up her soul and then leave her when you were finished."

He had to diffuse this somehow, another tactic. "Is that what happened to you?"

"The hell with you, with all of you. My great love, the man who promised me everything, who would love me forever, left me with nothing, a shell emptied out and then—" She'd stopped.

"Then what?" he asked calmly. It was important to find out what was driving her. Then, he might gain an edge.

She laughed bitterly, "If that wasn't enough, then I found myself here, lost on the other side. Apparently, taking your own life, even in desperation, is a great taboo. All I wanted was for my pain to stop, but it didn't. It didn't. But then I found Hallie, and I had a reason for being again."

He looked at the pitiful creature with a mixture of emotions. Obviously, there was more than anger here. There was anguish, fear, and so much despair. Maybe he was meant to do more. Maybe there was a way he could help. "Madeline, listen to me. There is more than this for you than just this cold, decaying place. You could move on to something better."

She was hunched over, her face covered by her hands. Her voice came out small and shaking, "Do you mean I could move into the light?"

He shrugged, a little uncertain. "Yes, things would be better for you if you moved on," and he added tentatively, "into the light."

And then, she let her hands slowly move away from her face, and she smiled wickedly through her tears. It was a whisper, "You first, Jack."

He recoiled from the change in her, "What?"

She flung back her lanky brown hair. Strangely, in a very peripheral way, she almost resembled Hallie. Her voice was strong and filled with glee. "I don't notice you in a big hurry to go into the light, Jack."

He cleared his throat and replied somewhat unconvincingly, "That's because I have a purpose here, a mission."

"To get rid of me?"

"To free Hallie of you."

"And once it's done, Jack. What then? Are you ready to bid your adieus to the flesh and move on without her?"

"Well, I guess I'll have to." He said with not nearly enough conviction.

"That doesn't sound very convincing for a hero, a knight in shining armor."

"I never claimed to be that." Damn, she had him on the defensive. This was no good.

She jumped on it, "Exactly, Jack, you're still a man with flaws and earthly desires." Then she bent in closer to him, so near he could smell a staleness emanating from her. "Let's make a deal, Jack. I used to work at a casino in Vegas. I saw the biggest high rollers around, and I think you're a high roller." Her, in Vegas? She must have changed a bit from those days.

He backed away, repulsed. "Maybe I used to be."

She laughed, "What's being noble going to get you today, Jack? Not your precious Hallie. Not the love you never had in your own life. But I can get that for you."

He stared into the green eyes that glared back at him as deceptive slits. She was a viper — the serpent dangling the tantalizing fruit inches from his starving mouth. "What are you talking about?" He asked regrettably.

She grinned. Seeing that delighted grin on the bony, little face was disturbing. "I thought you'd want to hear me out. You want a life with Hallie or the best you can get in your present state. And I want what I had, complete control of her writing. Let me live again through Sebastian Winters, and I'll give you Hallie in dream time."

He took a sharp breath, shaking his head. He didn't like this, but he couldn't stop asking, "What do you mean?"

"You can share a whole life together in her dreams. You can go anywhere, do anything." And then she lowered her voice tantalizingly, "You can even have a place together near the water and have the kids that she's always wanted. You can have it all, Jack, if you only share a little piece of her with me."

"Just the writing?"

She smiled again, evidently feeling more confident. "Yes and relinquish control over this book."

The coldness crept into him around his heart. Here comes the fine print. "What does that mean exactly?"

"You're a smart man, Jack. Samory must triumph, and your creation—"

"Jacob McFarin?"

"Must die." Then she tacked on matter-of-factly, "And Gabriella too. She betrayed him. She has to go."

He was silent. That moment in Madeline's dank little hell stretched into an eternity. All the players were there. He even had his own little devil tempting him, only asking for small pieces of his soul.

A dull ache thudded in his chest. He wanted to tell himself that Jacob and Gabriella were just made-up characters. In killing them, he wouldn't be betraying Hallie as well as snuffing out some part of his own life force. But deep down, that quiet voice within, the one he'd suppressed so effectively in life, told him there were laws at work here that he didn't understand.

Those little things like integrity and loyalty that he had brushed aside at inconvenient moments in his former life counted and made a difference in the big scheme of things.

That although it seemed like having Hallie was everything, the kind of man he was with Hallie counted for an awful lot, too. Staring into the cold green eyes, he saw his life that could have been swirling into the darkness beyond his reach. "So that's the offer, is it Maddie?"

Her eyes widened. She'd expected him to jump at the bait. He was sure of it. And most of him wanted to, but not all and not enough. "Yes, Jack, that's the deal. Take it or leave it."

He stood up and quietly said, "I'm afraid I'm going to have to leave it, Maddie."

Shock canvassed her pale face. At that moment, he felt truly sorry for her. She almost looked like a child, a poor, confused, lost child. She muttered frantically, "You can't."

"I can't subject Hallie to a life where she will be split between two undeserving ghosts. And that's what we are, just ghosts living in the past. I hope you can move on, Maddie, because I do believe there's more out there for you and maybe me too."

He brushed past her and walked over to the sleeping Hallie. He bent over to kiss her on the forehead before he drew her into his arms.

He sat beside her on the bed, watching her brush out her long brown hair, as he'd done countless times before. He knew now that he hadn't savored those moments enough or etched them deeply enough into his memory. He felt Aunt Marie's presence and looked up to see her standing in the doorway. She looked amazingly transformed, a woman of forty-five and more than a few pounds lighter. He smiled, "Aunt Marie, I had no idea what a looker you were."

She grinned, he thought, perhaps blushing a little. "My time here is finished, Jack. Hallie doesn't need me anymore."

He nodded, not wanting to voice the obvious. "It feels much better here. What happened to Madeline? Did she move on?"

"Yes, but not to a higher plane, just away from here, looking for another place to cling to until she's ready."

"Will she ever be ready?"

"For some, it takes a lot longer to learn."

He smiled grimly, "And maybe some of us don't want to accept what we've learned." He paused, "What about Hallie's writing now that Madeline's gone?"

"She took a little too much credit. Madeline didn't make Hallie a good writer, just a good writer of vampire novels. There are plenty of things to write about."

There was another question on his mind, but he was uncertain if he should even ask. "I made the right choice, didn't I? I mean about Madeline's offer."

"Well, you made a choice, and you'll have to live with it."

"Will you ever give me a straight answer?"

"Let's just say I'm very proud of you, Jack, and of the man you've become. And I know your Dad is, too."

He nodded, "Thanks, that means a lot to me."

Hallie crossed to the mirror and pulled her hair back into a barrette. He knew she didn't like to spend a lot of time fussing with it. There were too many other things on her mind. Even as he sat there, he could feel the pull away from here growing stronger and stronger. "You don't have much time left here, Jack."

"I know. But I've got to say goodbye to her. I think I'd rather face Madeleine in that awful place a hundred times over than do this."

"I know," she smiled, always with great compassion in her sparkling blue eyes. "But just remember, Jack. Remember to look for God's love in everything."

He shook his head. "I don't know what that means."

And then she was gone. Hallie stood staring at her reflection in the mirror, and then she stopped with her hands in mid-air, slowly turning around. There were tears in her eyes. He, in his heart, knew for the first time she could see him, really see him, not as a dream. "Jack," she whispered. "I always thought way in the back of my mind you weren't real, and I was just a little nuts."

"I think we're both probably a little nuts."

She smiled and sat down beside him. Her eyes glistened with joy, and then she saw something in his face and knew. "What's wrong?"

"I can't stay long, Hallie."

"I thought things were going well. I woke up this morning and felt so good that I thought—"

"I'm glad, Hallie. I want you to feel good, be happy and free."

He couldn't bring himself to say it. Concern marred her beautiful face, "What do you mean?"

"I want you to know that you're going to be just fine. You're the strongest woman I've ever known and—"

"Oh, Jack," her voice was choked up with tears. "You promised you'd find a way."

He swallowed, "There was a way, Hallie, but I couldn't sacrifice you. I don't want you living for someone else ever again."

"Damn you, why didn't you let me choose?"

"Because I know you, you would have given up yourself for us to be together, and I wouldn't let you do that. You're too important to me."

The tears were running down her cheeks. "It's not fair. There's so much we never got to do. I wanted, I wanted to see the ocean with you."

This was too much. It didn't seem right. He didn't understand it at all. All he did know was that the pull was becoming unbearable, too strong to resist.

"I have to go, Hallie. Know I love you. I always will."

He stood up and started toward the door. The last thing he heard was her whisper behind him, her prayer. "Please don't leave me, Jack." And then he was taken into the brightness.

Epilogue

He felt his head hit hard as it came down on the hot New York City pavement. There was scuffling around him, and images flooded in and out of his line of vision. He closed his eyes, and colors swirled beneath his eyelids, voices filtered in and out. "Come on. It looks like a mild head trauma."

"I saw him clutch his chest. Was it a heart attack?"

"Too early to tell. Step back, everyone."

"Would things be different, Jack, if you had another chance?"

He heard his own voice somewhere inside his head. *"But it's not possible."*

"My dear boy, haven't you learned yet that anything is possible? Absolutely anything."

And then another voice out of the darkness, "Is he going to be all right. I called you on my cell phone."

"Would you step back, Ma'am, please?"

"Yes, but could you please tell me where you're taking him. I just want to make sure he's all right."

His head was throbbing, but he managed to open his eyes. The blurriness cleared, just for a minute, and he saw the paramedics bending over him and then not far behind them. She looked at him with her soft, sweet, brown eyes filled with worry.

"If you had another chance, Jack, would it be different?"

"I'd be different, and I'd spend my life making her happy."

"You can follow us, Ma'am. We're headed to St. Vincent's."

She nodded. "I will," and repeated emphatically, "I will follow you."

Finis

More Books by Evelyn Klebert

The Lady in the Blue Dress
6 x 9 Softcover & Hardcover 214 pages
ISBN 978-1-61342-600-5
ISBN (Hardcover) 978-1-61342-418-6

When she was a child, Mika Devalieur was introduced to her grandmother's most precious possession — a priceless and mysterious painting that she simply called The Lady in the Blue Dress. Upon Adele St. Clair's death, the painting is left in the care of her granddaughter with only one stipulation. Mika must hand over the family heirloom to a total stranger. Mika Devalieur desperately wants to deny her beloved grandmother's last request, but she can't. Torn between her Gran's last wishes and her desire to hold onto the Lady, she ultimately journeys to rural Virginia, where an enigmatic man shows her that this painting is only the beginning.

What quickly becomes clear is that James Clairmont knows much more about her and the Lady than he is letting on. He begins to slowly unravel a powerful supernatural connection that spans three generations of her family. Mika finds herself desperate to uncover the entire truth before she falls in love with a man filled with so many secrets — secrets about him, about her, and most especially about The Lady in the Blue Dress. (First published on Kindle Vella, episodes 1-23.)

Dumaine Street
6 x 9 Softcover & Hardcover 306 pages
ISBN 978-1-61342-902-0
ISBN (Hardcover) 978-1-61342-416-2

Voices in her head, catastrophic emotions, hallucinations — Rebecca Wells is more than convinced that she is losing her mind. And as a last-ditch effort, she contacts a self-professed counselor who seems convinced he can help.

Gabriel Sutton has abandoned the world of medicine to navigate a realm filled with psychic phenomena. Diagnosing Becca with extreme empathic abilities, he struggles to help her stabilize her gifts while trying desperately not to fall in love with his patient.

From the realm of vulnerability into a crusade to use their profound gifts to rescue others from peril on the other side of death, these two follow an astonishing and unpredictable path into each other's hearts.

The Tethering
A Portent of Crows
6 x 9 Softcover & Hardcover 201 pages
ISBN 978-1-61342-599-2
ISBN (Hardcover) 978-1-61342-419-3

Deborah Brandt's beloved Aunt Gena always told her that she was special, a bit different, and would have to live her life, unlike other people. Of course, this she disregarded as the ramblings of her lovely but notably eccentric aunt. Although there were the things that Aunt Gena said that seemed true — like Deborah being sensitive to energy shifts, having potentially psychic impressions, and dreaming of a spirit guide — none of it could be real. But the most ridiculous thing that her Aunt Gena told her before she died was that someone special was out there for her. She said that he was an extraordinary man who was not only her perfect match but someone who she would learn from so that they could help the world in difficult times. How ridiculous! It sounds like a fairy tale, and no such person exists.

Daniel Wren is unique. He has been raised and trained from a young age to hone his psychic gifts. He lives in a world unimagined by most. And he has been waiting for years to contact his counterpart, soulmate, if you will. But the problem is that she is painfully unaware of the type of life that he lives and the life she would be entering into if they came together.

His dilemma becomes how best to proceed. How can he win her over and move forward before outside forces take that decision away from him?

Travels into the Breach
Accounts of a Reluctant Mystic
6 x 9 Softcover & Hardcover 171 pages
ISBN 978-1-61342-323-3
ISBN (Hardcover) 978-1-61342-417-9

At first glance, his life seems quiet, serene, and even uneventful. Malachi McKellan, a 65-year-old widower and author of esoteric books, lives largely as a recluse in a house situated just off the banks of Bayou St. John in New Orleans. But unbeknownst to most, he is also a bit of a detective, a specific kind of detective whose specialty is psychic attacks. Alongside his lifelong companion and spirit guide Simon Tull, a 19th-century, 20-something English gent, Malachi battles the unseen, and is an unacknowledged hero to the most vulnerable. Most of the population have no idea what is really happening beneath the surface of the world in which they live.

In this collection of adventures, Malachi McKellan and Simon Tull wage war against the most insidious elements of the paranormal. In *The Three*, Malachi and Simon come to the aid of a young woman being victimized by a group of dark witches. An old apartment building is the scene of an unimaginable battle against monstrous forces in *The Lost Soul*. Malachi and Simon find themselves strategizing against a psychic vampire in *Obsession*, and *The Hotel* turns back time to the 1980s where Malachi confronts a demonic spirit. In *Between*, a past life is revisited as Malachi attempts to rescue a beloved sister from committing her existence to vengeance, and *The Wedding* takes a personal turn when Malachi must confront painful truths while endeavoring to protect his niece from a potentially devastating union.

Travel into the breach with a pair of paranormal warriors who choose to confront overwhelming forces on a battlefield unsuspected by most.

Gravier's Bookshop
A New Orleans Paranormal Mystery (#1)
6 x 9 Softcover & Hardcover 172 pages
ISBN 978-1-61342-288-5
ISBN (Hardcover) 978-1-61342-411-7

Max Gravier had no intention of becoming a recluse, but after his wife's death it seems his life is heading in that direction. He spends his time running Gravier's Bookshop on Magazine Street and occasionally on the quiet helps the police solve a crime with his psychic sensitivities. That is until he answers Caroline Breslin's call, a cry for help out of his dreams that draws him into a fierce battle for a young woman's soul.

In this first installment of The New Orleans Paranormal Mystery series, Caroline Breslin, an amazingly gifted empath, is determined to strike out on her own and has moved out from the protection of her family home. All is going extremely well until, of course, she comes under siege from a devastating supernatural attack. The last thing Caroline wants is to run back to her family for help, even though she is painfully in over her head. What she really needs is a knight in shining armor — or maybe just that guy that keeps haunting her dreams.

Join them and the whole Breslin family psychic clan in this first installment of The New Orleans Paranormal Mystery Series where you'll travel into a new world just a few steps into the turbulent realm of the unseen.

The Hotel Mandolin
A New Orleans Paranormal Mystery (#2)
6 x 9 Softcover & Hardcover 146 pages
ISBN 978-1-61342-290-8
ISBN (Hardcover) 978-1-61342-412-4

Peril is wrapped up in the most enticing of disguises in *The Hotel Mandolin*, the second installment of The New Orleans Paranormal Mystery series. It's opulent, classic, and one of the most renowned hotels nestled deep in New Orleans' famous business district, but something is amiss at The Hotel Mandolin.

PI Peter Norfleet is calling out the big guns to help him investigate a recent suicide at the famous establishment — his good friend Max Gravier, a formidable psychic, and his girlfriend, Caroline Breslin, a talented empath. But none of them can seem to scratch the surface of this puzzle, no one except Cassie Breslin, Caroline's clairvoyant mother, who has somehow tapped into an unexpected connection with a tragic ghost from the turn of the century. And the more she uncovers, the more dangerous and malevolent the mystery becomes

The House at Pritchard Place
A New Orleans Paranormal Mystery (#3)
6 x 9 Softcover & Hardcover 138 pages
ISBN 978-1-61342-292-2
ISBN (Hardcover) 978-1-61342-413-1

Nothing is really wrong with the old Warrick House on Dante St. except that there most certainly is. Nothing is exactly wrong with its new mysterious owner except that Elise is sure that something doesn't add up. It isn't obvious, but sometimes the most dangerous things aren't.

In the third installment of The New Orleans Paranormal Mystery series, with the help of her very psychic sister and her children, the Breslin clan, Elise Ashford is about to embark on a wild rescue mission straight into another dimension that will land her squarely somewhere she doesn't expect, right back into her past. She'll land full circle; in a childhood home whose memory still haunts her to this day -- *The House at Pritchard Place*.

Treading on Borrowed Time
6 x 9 Softcover & Hardcover 223 pages
ISBN 978-1-61342-214-4
ISBN (Hardcover)

For Julia Moreau, life seems complicated. Emerging from a failed marriage and managing a lifetime of diabetes, she lives alone in her childhood home where she communicates with the spirit of her Great Aunt Lilia. But Julia doesn't have a clue what complicated is until she is thrust into being the key chess piece in a match between two powerful men of extraordinary abilities on the wild hunt for a mystical creature hidden in the heart of

New Orleans' French Quarter. Will Julia lose her soul to the karma of a devastating past life or her heart to the love of a man driven by dark forces? What is clear is that whichever way she turns she is *Treading on Borrowed Time.*

Sanctuary of Echoes
6 x 9 Softcover & Hardcover 371 pages
ISBN 978-1-61342-211-3
ISBN (Hardcover) 978-1-61342-409-4

Ghosts unacknowledged do not sleep.

Corey Knight has resigned herself to a quiet, reclusive life spent living out the rest of her days in her childhood home on the fringes of New Orleans' French Quarter. But the unexpected specter of her deceased father plunges her into a mad quest for a missing supernatural weapon unearthed long ago. And un-fortunately, her only ally is a lost love she once betrayed.

Iain Shaw returns to New Orleans, a city he abandoned a decade before while fleeing a devastating past. Here, he is forced to confront it again in the visage of the woman he once adored - one that he is now determined to get back at any cost.

Follow them both in a wild paranormal tale of discovery and redemption as they confront and unearth the echoes of a buried and unyielding truth that once tore them irreparably apart.

More Books by Evelyn Klebert

A Quiet Moment
6 x 9 Softcover & Hardcover 273 pages
ISBN 978-1-61342-326-4
ISBN (Hardcover) 978-1-61342-435-3

Jacob Wyss is caught in a rut, in fact on the verge of being engulfed by it. After an excruciating and disillusioning divorce, his life as an artist in a sleepy-college town at the foot of the Appalachian Mountains has become quiet, routine, and maddening in its predictability. One wintry day, his deep restlessness drives him out in precarious conditions to a largely empty bookstore nearly devoid of another living soul, nearly.

Aimee Marston isn't like everyone else. On the surface, she lives a sedate life working as a feature writer for a small local newspaper in addition to several other editorial jobs to help make ends meet. But just beneath, her existence is largely not her own. She is a sensitive, an empathetic psychic, guided by her calling to use her gifts to help others. Unfortunately, as a result, her secretiveness has made her defensive, protective of herself, and prevented her from having much of a life.

A psychic call for help sends Aimee out on a freezing January morning where her destiny and Jacob's collide sending both their lives spiraling onto an unexpected and often disturbing track. Two lonely souls connect, not by accident, but by design. Theirs is the intersection of two spiritual paths, two lovers who must struggle to overcome the phantoms of a past life, as well as the challenges of their own inner demons to carve out an extraordinary future together.

More Books by Evelyn Klebert

Dragonflies - Journeys into the Paranormal
6 x 9 Softcover & Hardcover 176 pages
ISBN 978-1-88756-072-6
ISBN (Hardcover) 979-8-32548-418-6

In every form of creation, there is a blueprint for living, for experience, for interpretation. In flight, they can twist, turn, alter direction, pause in midair, and even fly backward. The dragonfly is the master of adaptability. They are a living prism, refracting light, and color, seemingly shifting their essence.

The lesson the dragonfly gives is that life is never what it appears to be.

In "The Wizard," as a novice practitioner of magic, Aurora Finn finds herself battling against the illusions of a powerful wizard intent on separating her from the world she knows. "The Sojourners" is a gentle story of a mother and daughter whose tenancy in an old Virginia farmhouse uncovers the trials and sorrows of its former occupants. A bookstore clerk gets an extraordinary customer on Halloween night in "Late One Night at Berstrums Books." In "The Tear," a woman coping with her fatal illness unknowingly begins a track on a mystical journey that will entirely restructure her vision of the world.

These stories follow the path of the dragonfly imbued with the momentum and energy of change, taking a winding and treacherous journey that ultimately leads to truth buried beneath perception.

Breaking Through the Pale
6 x 9 Softcover 134 pages
ISBN 978-1-88756-045-0

Journey with metaphysical author Evelyn Klebert into a collection of short stories that travel beyond the pale into the unpredictable realm of the paranormal.

In "A Grey Mourning," a disillusioned man encounters a mysterious being on the foggy streets of New Orleans. "Contact" is a tale of automatic writing, when a young artist establishes communication with a spirit guide, and the victim of a car crash unravels the true nature of her existence in "Dancing on the Threshold." The final tale is called "Isolation," in which a confused and disoriented woman finds herself in an old, quaint house where she must piece together the mystical implications surrounding her predicament.

Explanations
6 x 9 Softcover 82 pages
ISBN 978-1-93493-515-6

In this, her second poetry collection, Evelyn Klebert takes us down the intricate path of a personal journey. Life with its particular struggles, pitfalls, and ultimately triumphs clearly begins to mirror a universal path, the quest for answers that we all ultimately pursue. In this reflective, esoteric collection we can all explore and seek some of life's elemental mysteries and hopefully when all is said and done emerge with some *Explanations*.

More Books by Evelyn Klebert

The Witches' Own
6 x 9 Softcover & Hardcover 140 pages
ISBN 978-1-61342-058-4
ISBN (Hardcover) 978-1-61342-428-5

On the surface things seem quiet and serene in the pictur-esque coastal village of Kilmarnock, Virginia. But something unseen roams its lush forests as the past and present collide and the unthinkable begins to wreak its vengeance. Young Lucy Bonner is executed for witchcraft in the town's distant and bru-tal past. Her death triggers an unholy chain of events which grasp at the restless heart of novelist Peter McQuade, spurring him towards a quest to uncover the dark and terrifying truth.

The Left Palm
And Other Halloween Tales of the Supernatural
6 x 9 Softcover 117 pages
ISBN 978-1-93493-556-9

Halloween is the time of year when that veil between worlds is thinned, and you can just catch a quick glimpse into the realm of the unknowable. In this collection of short stories, Evelyn Klebert takes you to a place where ordinary life splinters into the sphere of the paranormal.

The journey begins with one woman's unstoppable quest for vengeance against a supernatural creature in "Wolves" and continues in an old historical graveyard where a horrifying dis-covery is uncovered in "Emma Fallon." In "The Soul Shredder," a psychiatrist's unusual patient opens his eyes to a disturbing new view of reality, while in "Wildflowers," a woman strikes up a supernatural friendship with impossible implications. And in

"The Left Palm," a fortuneteller in the French Quarter receives a most unexpected and terrifying customer.

White Harbor Road
And Other Tales of Paranormal Romance
6 x 9 Softcover 130 pages
ISBN 978-1-61342-066-9

A psychic soul mate, a time traveler, a horror writer, and an enigmatic stranger take a selection of resilient, life-battered heroines to a place of paranormal healing and transformation. In this collection of short stories, *White Harbor Road* is the last stop where life's burdens and hardships evolve into something unexpected.

The Broken Vow
Vol. I of The Clandestine Exploits of a Werewolf
6 x 9 Softcover & Hardcover 204 pages
ISBN 978-1-61342-133-8
ISBN (Hardcover) 978-1-61342-420-9

In the heart of every man there is a history. In the heart of every monster there is a story. In this first installment of *The Clandestine Exploits of a Werewolf*, Ethan Garraint is on a vendetta that begins in the heart of the Pyrenees with the fall of Montségur and leads him to the streets of New Orleans nearly five hundred years later. But the person he chases isn't really a man anymore and Ethan has been a werewolf for almost a millennium. With the aid of a gifted seer, he is on a blood hunt that will culminate in a journey that crosses the line between heaven and earth and ends somewhere in between.

More Books by Evelyn Klebert

Considerations
6 x 9 Softcover 68 pages
ISBN 978-1-88756-062-7

Sometimes the struggle to understand the meaning and complexities of living comes down to a single moment of introspection or a fleeting yet meaningful reflection. This collection of poetry by Evelyn Klebert takes you down a winding path of self-discovery where the resolution may not always be absolute, but the journey is indeed unforgettable. It a wide and varied map of inspired poetry for your examination and consideration.

Appointment with the Unknown
The Hotel Stories
6 x 9 Softcover & Hardcover 155 pages
ISBN 978-1-61342-360-8
ISBN (Hardcover) 978-1-61342-421-6

A hotel, for most, represents a normal place, a predictable realm of commonality. One might even go as far to say a safe space, the reliable where nothing particularly unusual is expected to happen. Or is it? Dimensional traveling, spirit guides, mystical storms, and soul mates separated by time are only a few elements dotting this supernatural landscape. Drop into a collection of romantic paranormal stories where that place of commonality is only the threshold, the jumping-off point, for extraordinary adventures into the unknown.

Visit Evelyn's website at:
www.evelynklebert.com
Cornerstone Book Publishers
www.cornerstonepublishers.com